FAITH'S LOVE

AMISH WEDDING SEASON

BOOK 3

SAMANTHA PRICE

D1366490

FAITH'S LOVE

Copyright © 2014, 2015 Samantha Price

All Rights Reserved

Second Edition 2015

License Notes

ISBN-13: 978-1499542110

Contents

CHAPTER 1

I am crucified with Christ: nevertheless I live; yet not

I, but Christ liveth in me: and the life which I now

live in the flesh I live by the faith of the Son of God,

who loved me, and gave himself for me.

Galatians 2:20

"Thank you for being my attendant, Faith." Lilly giggled and corrected herself. "I mean bridesmaid. The *Englisch* call them bridesmaids, don't they?"

"*Jah*, I'm going to be a bridesmaid. *Denke* for asking me," Faith said.

Lilly uncovered the bridesmaid's dress she had made for her dear friend, Faith, to wear at the wedding.

Faith helped Lilly pull the calico cover off the

dress to get a better look. "Oh, it's lovely," Faith said. She had tried it on for a fitting some time ago, but this was the first time she had seen it finished and ready to wear. She held it up against herself. "How does it look?"

"It looks lovely. It's such a nice color for you."

The dress was a deep purple shade and was in an Amish style rather than a traditional bridesmaid's dress.

Faith laid the dress across the bed. She wished that Lilly had a mirror in her room, but Lilly's parents didn't believe in having mirrors in the *haus*, considering that it led to vanity and pride.

"Do your *mamm* and *dat* feel better about you marrying Jason?" Faith asked.

Lilly slumped onto her bed. "*Jah*, they said it was up to me and it's my choice which world I want to live in. Of course they would have preferred me to marry an Amish *mann*."

"I think they're just happy that you aren't moving back to Long Island with him."

"I suppose so, but they would be happier if Jason was Amish and living in the community." Lilly turned her head to stare out the small window that overlooked the farm. "I never imagined that I would have just a civil service and not an Amish wedding. It seems a little strange to be having such a small *Englisch* wedding with hardly any guests."

"Don't worry; your wedding will be so special. You're going to marry someone you truly love and he's a *wunderbaar* person. That can only be a fine thing."

Lilly's shoulders drooped down as her eyes were drawn back to her friend. "I know. It's just that I've always assumed I would marry and live in the community. I never even considered that I might have a wedding that wasn't Amish."

Faith licked her lips while she tried to think of something else encouraging to say. "Don't keep thinking that way, Lilly. Enjoy your wedding as it is. It might even be better than an Amish wedding and even better than you ever imagined."

Lilly straightened her back. "*Denke,* that's true. I'll have to think more positively." Lilly's attention turned to the dress on the bed as she checked the sewing in a couple of places.

"This isn't the first time you're meeting Jason's parents, is it?

"*Nee,* they came here a few weeks ago to meet me."

Faith lifted up a corner of the plastic cover over

Lilly's wedding dress, which was hanging on a clothes peg. "I certainly love the feel of your dress. It's so soft and silky."

Lilly stood up and lifted the wedding dress out of its covering. "Is it a little too *Englisch*?"

Faith studied the dress. The fabric was silky with just the hint of a shine; the style was very modest with a high neckline and long sleeves. The hem of Lilly's wedding dress finished just below the knee. It was slightly more fitted than any Amish dress Faith had ever seen. "*Jah*, it's white like the *Englisch* wedding dresses, but it's still a little Amish in the style."

Lilly tipped her head to one side as she re-examined her dress. "I've tried to have something that is in between the two worlds, a little Amish and a little *Englisch*." Still gazing at her dress, she said, "I don't think that Jason will ever want to live in the Amish world."

"Has that been on your mind a lot?"

Lilly nodded slowly without taking her eyes off her dress.

"You never know what can happen." Faith knew that Lilly was more than a little disappointed that Jason wasn't Amish so she changed the subject. "I can't believe you're getting married tomorrow."

"Neither can I." Lilly's eyes lit up at the mention of her marriage. "It was very nice of your father not to charge us for booking out the restaurant."

"He said that's the least he could do since you've been such a good employee for so many years. I think you're his favorite worker—favorite person, maybe."

Lilly giggled. "Do you think so?"

Faith nodded.

Lilly and Jason had reserved Faith's parents'

restaurant, where both Lilly and Faith worked, for the wedding.

The whole time Faith was up in Lilly's bedroom looking at the dresses, she was also listening out for Lilly's *bruder*, Ben, in the *haus*. So far, she had heard nothing. *I wonder if he comes home for lunch,* she thought. Faith had been keen on Ben for some time, but he had never shown any sign of being interested in her.

Lilly picked the bridesmaid's dress off the bed and handed it to Faith. "Try the dress on. There's still time to make some changes if it doesn't fit right."

"Really? The night before the wedding is enough time?"

Lilly smiled and nodded.

"You're lucky to be such a good sewer."

"It's just practice, that's all. I used to help *mamm* sew all our dresses. I've had plenty of practice," Lilly said.

Faith pulled her modest Amish dress off over her head and carefully tried on the bridesmaid's dress. "It feels nice. How does it look?"

Lilly straightened the dress, then stepped back a few paces and studied her friend. "*Jah*, it looks lovely and I don't think I need to do anything to it."

"I'll take it off. I'm nervous with it on, in case I rip it accidently or something."

Lilly laughed. "That's probably best."

Faith put her arms straight over her head and Lilly carefully lifted the purple bridesmaid dress over her friend's head.

Lilly put her head to the side and stared at Faith, who was busy putting back on her Amish dress. "Verity's over at the restaurant now, arranging the tables and doing the decorations. You don't mind sitting next to Ben, do you?"

"I'll be sitting next to Ben at the reception?" Faith straightened her dress and adjusted her prayer *kapp*.

"*Jah*, right next to him." Lilly giggled and sat back on the bed.

Faith could not stop the smile that tugged at the corner of her lips. *I'll be sitting next to Ben the whole time. Maybe he'll notice me now. He'll have to speak to me if I'm sitting right next to him*, she thought. "Lilly, I told you no matchmaking. I should never have told you I like him."

"I've been very careful about not doing that, and it's not matchmaking. It's where the two of you would be sitting anyway even if you hadn't told me you're madly in love with him." Lilly had a wicked gleam in her eye.

Faith decided to ignore Lilly's exaggeration about

being madly in love with Ben. "All right, then. I suppose you're off the hook this time. But remember, no matchmaking—and under no circumstances may you tell him that I like him."

Lilly expelled a deep breath. "Well, all right then, but I do think you need to make a move."

Faith tipped her head to the side. "What do you mean?"

"Drop some hints, let him know that you like him. Give him a little encouragement."

Faith shook her head emphatically. "*Nee,* I want him to do all that. I want him to chase me; that would be more romantic."

Lilly pushed her lips together tightly. "I know of at least two girls in the community who are interested in him and I don't want you to miss out on a *gut mann* like my *bruder.*"

"I appreciate you telling me that, but I'm not going to throw myself at a man; he has to be interested in *me*." Faith gave a quick nod of her head to emphasize her point.

Lilly pursed her lips tightly again and this time jutted them out in a show of disapproval at what Faith had just said.

* * *

As Faith walked home from Lilly's *haus*, she hoped that Ben would make some sort of a move, invite her somewhere, offer to take her home from a singing—something. Since she had liked him for quite a while, she was desperate for some sign from him that he felt the same.

Faith was the youngest of five girls and the others

had all married, leaving her the last one at home. She was pleased to have a lot more peace and quiet at her home with all her sisters now living elsewhere, but the bad part was she had more chores. Faith certainly did not feel in a hurry to get married like some of the other girls her age in the community. She was nearly twenty years of age and girls in the community started to look around for a husband from the age of seventeen or eighteen. Some considered it old to get married at twenty. The more Faith thought about it, the more she considered that Lilly was trying to push her a little too hard to get Ben to notice her.

"Faith."

A manly voice rang in Lilly's ears and she turned to see Ben walking toward her from the fields. For some reason she had not even thought to look for him as she walked away. "Hello, Ben."

"Were you just visiting Lilly?"

His clothes were covered in a fine layer of dust and his cheeks and forehead had smears of dirt on them, but that did nothing to detract from his handsome looks.

"*Jah*, just trying on the dress for her wedding."

Ben smiled at Faith and said, "How have you been?"

"I've been well." Faith's eyes dropped to the ground. It was an awkward exchange and she did not know what to say to him. She wanted to lean toward him and wipe the smudges on his face with her fingers, but she was not close enough with him to do that and he would surely consider the gesture too forward. She summoned a little boldness, though, and looked up into his clear blue eyes. "You have a little dirt on your face."

Ben laughed. "Do I? Oh, no, where?" He dusted his hand against his pants and brushed at his face with his fingertips.

"Well, just there, and there." Faith pointed to the dirt on his face and couldn't help but laugh at his comical reaction.

"Is that better," he said, after he had made several attempts to wipe the smudges away.

Faith smiled and shook her head. "You've made it worse."

"Wipe them off for me, then." He leaned in close toward her.

Little tingles of pleasure ran up and down Faith's body before she even touched his face with her fingers. She knew in that moment he must like her a little. "There, all gone."

"*Denke*. I've been cleaning out the buggies this

morning; I guess I must have rubbed my face when my hands were grubby."

Faith recalled how he had changed in the last few years. Both he and his twin, Esther, had light blonde hair when they were younger, and now Ben's hair had turned dark brown, whereas Esther's had stayed blonde. The dark brown hair highlighted his clear blue eyes perfectly against his sun-darkened skin. *He's not only handsome and kind; he's very masculine and polite, as well,* Faith thought. *He's also funny.*

"Well, I guess I'll see you at the wedding," Ben said.

Ben was known for being quiet and shy and it appeared that both he and Faith had run out of things to say.

"Okay, bye." Faith gave a nod of her head and started walking again. She was glad at least that he had made the effort to come over and talk to her. Surely that meant that he liked her. He could perhaps have found something more to talk about; he didn't really say much at all. *He could have invited me somewhere,* she thought. *We were alone with no one around; it would have been a perfect opportunity.*

The October wind was getting a little chilly and Faith wished that she had remembered to wear her coat. Her nose felt numb to the touch; the only thing warm were her feet, which were wrapped in thick socks inside her black lace-up boots. *I'll go get a ride home with dat.* It was nearly time for her father to finish at the restaurant and it was closer than her home, which meant less walking.

He usually finished at four p.m. every day except Sunday, when the restaurant was closed. When Faith walked past the front of the restaurant, she could see that there were only a couple of tables occupied. Mid afternoon was always quiet in the restaurant.

Faith decided to go through the back entrance rather than walk through the front doors. When she rounded the corner of the building, she saw her father leaning on the red, brick wall near the door.

CHAPTER 2

I beseech you therefore, brethren, by the mercies of God, that ye present your bodies a living sacrifice, holy, acceptable unto God, which is your reasonable service.

Romans 12:1

"Are you all right, *Dat?*" Her father was always so full of energy, but now he looked exhausted and his usually ruddy complexion was a pale shade of gray.

"*Jah,* just tired, that's all."

Faith was immediately concerned that he had gasped for air as he spoke. "Well, what have you been doing?"

He took a while to answer and finally said slowly, "Probably too much." He took a shallow breath. "I'll be all right in a minute."

Faith stood staring at him, as she had no idea what to do; she just knew something was not right. "Do you want a drink of water?"

He shook his head. "I'll be heading home soon." He took some more shallow breaths. "Are you coming with me?"

"*Jah*, I'll just go inside for a minute. I'll drive the buggy." Faith went straight inside the doors of the restaurant and found Shane, the chef. "Shane, do you know what's wrong with my father?"

Shane was noisily chopping things and looked up when he heard Faith's voice. "Hi, Faith. I don't know; he's just not himself today. I think he's been overdoing things. Might need a vacation."

"He looks awful." Faith bit her bottom lip.

Shane placed his knife down on the chopping

board. "Should he go to a doctor?"

"No, I mean he probably should go, but he doesn't like doctors." Faith was more than a little concerned; she could not even remember her father ever being sick. "I'll get him home."

"Yeah, good idea. Tell him to take some time off. We can handle things here." Shane motioned in a circle with his hand.

"I'll try and get him to take some time off. It might be hard, though; you know what he's like. He says he's all right. Thanks, Shane."

Faith returned to her father, who was still in the same spot, leaning against the brick wall. She took his arm and walked him to the horse and buggy. He walked quite slowly, almost feebly.

Under normal circumstances, he would never have allowed Faith to drive the buggy while he rode as a passenger. He always insisted on doing the driving, but today he did not even make a whimper of a complaint when Faith insisted that she would drive.

During work hours, the buggy was unhitched and the horse kept in a makeshift stable behind the restaurant. As Faith hitched the buggy by herself, she was surprised that her father offered no help or even any advice on how to do it. Faith knew from this that he must have been feeling dreadful.

Once they were home, Faith's *mamm* ordered him straight to bed and made him some chicken broth.

Faith's *mamm* spooned the broth from a saucepan into a large soup bowl. "What do you think is wrong with him? He seemed all right this morning before he went in."

Faith cut two slices from the loaf of bread that her *mamm* had made earlier that day. "I've no idea. Could be a virus or something. I hear that they can hit a person pretty quickly."

Her *mamm* pulled out a chair from the kitchen table and sat down in it. She hung her head and put her elbows on the table. "Maybe that's all, but he never gets sick."

Faith tried not to show it, but she was more concerned than she was letting on. "I know. I'm sure he'll be over it by tomorrow. Don't worry."

"I hope he'll be over it tomorrow. Take the broth up on that tray over there, will you, Faith?"

"Sure." Faith arranged the broth, the bread, and a little bottle of hot sauce on the tray. Her father loved hot sauce with everything.

Faith placed the tray on the night table next to her father's bed. "How are you feeling?"

The gray tone was still evident on his face and he

was lying very still. She put her hand on his forehead and he felt to be a normal temperature.

"I'm all right." His speech was slower than usual.

"*Dat*, I know you are not feeling all right."

"I'm a bit off, but I'll be better in the morning. Just need a full night's sleep and some of your *mamm's* soup."

"Well, let me know if you need anything else."

Faith fluffed up his pillows and when he sat upright in bed, Faith placed the tray of food on his lap.

"Thanks, Faith. This looks very *wunderbaar*."

"Do you think you need a doctor?"

"*Nee*, of course not. *Gott* in heaven looks after me, not a man of this world." Her father picked up a piece of bread and ripped off a small chunk.

Faith was a little amused that he found the strength to say such a long sentence so emphatically.

He has an appetite so that must be a gut thing, she thought. "Okay, *Dat.* It's no shame to get a doctor, though. Many people in the community go to the doctor."

"I'll hear no more talk of doctors, Faith."

Faith could see that her talk of doctors was starting to cause him concern and stress. "All right. I'll talk no more of them."

Faith left her father to eat his soup in peace. She knew it was useless to press him further about seeing a doctor. Maybe he would be better in the morning.

* * *

Lilly and Jason's wedding ceremony was to be held in the back garden of the B&B. There were only fifty guests who would attend the ceremony and the reception, so the space in the garden was ideal, being not too big and not too small. The guests were made up of Jason's parents, the restaurant staff, and only Lilly's close family members. Jason's brother wasn't even there; neither were any of Jason's friends.

Verity had put a lot of work into the garden once she knew that Lilly wanted to have her wedding there. She had planted many roses, but unfortunately, they weren't in bloom due to the time of year. Knowing that Lilly loved roses, Jason had sourced pots of pink and white blooming roses, which were placed around the perimeter of the garden.

Verity and her husband worked tirelessly on the decorations of the restaurant and the garden for the big day. Fifty white chairs were placed in rows with an aisle up the middle where Lilly would walk to meet Jason. Long-stemmed white roses were held together with big, white bows, which framed the walkway up the aisle.

Both Lilly and Faith had stayed in a room at the B&B overnight.

Faith put her head out the window. "Oh, Lilly, look how lovely it is down there."

Lilly pushed Faith aside and looked out the window. "It's beautiful. I'm so happy; everything is working out perfectly."

"Will we put our dresses on now?"

"*Jah*, we should, I suppose."

It was half an hour before the ceremony was to start.

"Faith, your family has been so nice to me."

Faith giggled. "You're like one of our *familye* ever since you came to work at the restaurant. You've been like another *schweschder* to both Verity and me."

"*Jah*, like you need another one." Lilly laughed

because there were already five girls in Verity and Faith's family.

"Always room for one more," Faith said.

"Is your father all right? I heard he went home sick the other day."

"He's fine now. It was strange how he came over quite ill and then the next day he was okay. It could've been a nasty virus or something like that."

"As long as he's okay now, that's the main thing."

Faith nodded and pulled her purple bridesmaid's dress over her head. This time there was a mirror to look in. The dress wasn't very different from the Amish dresses she always wore, except that it was a little tighter in the fit. Once she put on her prayer *kapp*, she realized she would not look much different than she did every other day. She was a little disappointed, but tried not to show it. Faith was hoping she would get to dress up a little and wear something a little more *Englisch* than this dress.

Lilly's voice cut through her thoughts. "Do you like it?"

"*Jah*, I love it." Faith turned away from the mirror to see if Lilly had on her wedding dress. "Oh, wow. That looks beautiful on you. You look beautiful— stunning, even."

Faith stepped away from the mirror so Lilly could see herself.

"Oh, I look so different. I'm going to put on a little makeup."

"Really? Makeup?"

"Just a little concealer, base, and a touch of mascara. Jason doesn't like a lot of makeup, anyway." Lilly studied her own face in the mirror. "I'm just trying to hide a few flaws and make my skin look good, that's all. I don't want to look like a painted lady, or a lady of the night."

Faith giggled at Lilly's choice of words as she watched her pull out a few tubes from a little silver and purple cosmetic bag.

Lilly carefully applied the makeup, finishing off with a little lip-gloss. "How does it look?"

"Lovely, just lovely." Faith saw that Lilly's makeup looked very natural and no one would be able to see that she was wearing any at all except for the fact that her lips looked a shade darker than normal and very shiny. "Just don't turn into an *Englischer.*"

"I guess that's what I am, but my idea is to turn Jason Amish." Lilly reached on top of the wardrobe where she had stored her veil. She unwrapped it from the pale blue tissue paper that surrounded it. Three layers of white tulle tumbled out to the floor. Faith picked it up, unfolded it, and pushed the attached two-combed headpiece into Lilly's hair. The headpiece was a band of flowers made from small pearls with tiny diamantes in the center of each cluster.

"Just look at you!"

"Oh." Lilly put her hand over her mouth and giggled. "This looks so funny, very *Englisch.*"

"Jason will love to see you look like this."

"I hope so."

CHAPTER 3

*For by grace are ye saved through faith; and that not
of yourselves: it is the gift of God:*

Ephesians 2:8

By the time they reached the little garden where Lilly
was to be married, they were ten minutes late. Faith
peered out the glass doors at the back of the
restaurant, into the garden with a nervous Lilly
breathing down her neck. Faith saw that everyone was
seated in the white chairs. Jason was standing up in the
front with the marriage celebrant and all was ready to
go.

"All right, Lilly."

Both girls swung around to see Lilly's father.

"By *Englisch* tradition, I am to walk you down the

aisle to Jason."

"*Denke, Dat.*" Lilly gave Faith a big smile and linked her arm through her father's.

When Faith opened the glass doors to the garden, music from a string quartet in the corner of the garden sounded. Faith fought back tears; it was all so lovely. It wasn't Amish, but still it was special. She was sure that Lilly would look back with fondness on this special day—her wedding day.

Faith followed behind Lilly and stood to the side of her, once Lilly stood next to Jason. Faith looked over at Ben, who was standing beside Jason. Jason looked handsome and very different in the tight-fitting, dark gray *Englisch* formal suit.

The marriage celebrant was non-denominational, which was the choice of both Lilly and Jason. Lilly did not see the point of getting married by someone of another religion if she could not get married by the Amish bishop. Lilly left the Amish to be with Jason. Lilly confided often to Faith that she hoped that one day Jason would see the benefit of joining the community.

Faith considered that it must have been very hard for Lilly not to have an Amish wedding and to marry someone who was not Amish. Jason had come to believe in *Gott* and Lilly was most excited about that.

Faith took another glance at Ben and he turned slightly and caught her eye. Faith quickly looked away. *Was he looking at me? I wonder if he likes me. I wish he wasn't so shy. I don't want to be the one to make the first move.* Faith remembered that Lilly had said that she should make a move. Lilly would be well aware how shy her *bruder* was, so perhaps Faith should take her friend's advice, even though to do so would be against Faith's better judgment. Maybe she could try a tiny move or make a small suggestion, but only if he didn't do anything soon.

The celebrant pronounced that Jason and Lilly were man and wife. Jason gave Lilly a small kiss on the lips and everyone clapped. On Lilly's insistence, there was no exchange of rings as she was determined to keep to the Amish ways and tradition as much as she possibly could.

Faith could not control her eyes from straying again to Ben. He caught her gaze with a smile a number of times. The last time their eyes met, Ben held her gaze for quite some time before she looked away.

After the bride and groom greeted everyone, they made their way to the restaurant, which had been converted to a beautiful bridal reception room. Lilly asked that no photos be taken, but Jason persuaded her to let his parents take a couple of photos.

Covers of white fabric, secured at the back by large, white satin bows, transformed all the wooden restaurant chairs. The old wooden tables were covered in crisp, white linen tablecloths. Each table had a centerpiece made from large white feathers and huge white silk lilies. The ceiling was covered in white fabric, which softly billowed to give the appearance of being in a tent in some faraway place. Little white fairy lights were dotted throughout the ceiling and down every wall.

Just to the side of the bridal table was the four-tiered white wedding cake, which was made by Jason's mother.

Professional caterers and serving staff were employed, as all the restaurant and B&B staff were guests at the wedding.

Faith took her seat next to Lilly at the bridal table, which faced out toward all the other tables in the room. She looked over at her *mamm* and *dat* and was pleased to see that her *dat* was looking somewhat better—normal color had returned to his face.

There were many traditions of *Englisch* weddings that Faith had never experienced before; there was the first waltz, the speeches, and the throwing of the bouquet.

Lilly carried three cream roses with little feathered sprigs of white flowers surrounding the roses as a bouquet.

The main course was a choice of braised chicken and vegetables or steak with salad and baked jacket potatoes. For dessert, there were cheese platters and mixed plates of cheesecake. Chocolate cakes were placed on each table. Coffee was served after dinner, as were dark chocolates with soft creamy centers.

Faith considered that the food was delicious but not as plentiful as at an Amish wedding.

"How did you like the food, Faith?"

This was the first time that Ben had said anything to her right through the whole reception even though he was sitting right next to her. At least now she would not have to be the one to speak first. "I loved the food. What about you?"

"*Jah*, it was mighty fine."

Faith didn't know what else to say to him so she looked straight ahead.

Ben leaned in toward her and said in a low voice, "You look lovely today."

Faith glanced at him sideways and giggled a little. "*Denke*, Ben."

"Would you allow me to drive you home tonight?"

Faith's heart beat right out of her chest. When she got her breathing under control, she simply said, *"Jah."* She wondered if he could tell how much her face was beaming. She was sure she was simply glowing.

Faith had never been in Ben's buggy before, but she realized that he may have hoped to drive her home; otherwise, he would have come in his family's buggy. The thought of Ben planning to drive her home put a permanent smile on Faith's face. He has noticed me after all. I'm so glad, she thought.

Lilly had often hinted to Faith that some other girls had their eyes on Ben, so Faith was pleased that he had finally shown her some interest.

After a four-hour reception and a quick cutting of the wedding cake, Lilly and Jason left for their honeymoon. They were off to New York for two weeks so Jason could show Lilly the life he had had prior to meeting her.

Amish honeymoons were spent visiting relatives and were very different from *Englisch* honeymoons, which were more of a vacation with just the husband and wife.

Faith turned to Ben. "I'll have to tell *mamm* and *dat* I won't be home for a while."

Ben nodded. "I'll wait outside."

CHAPTER 4

*And be not conformed to this world: but be ye
transformed by the renewing of your mind, that ye may
prove what is that good, and acceptable, and perfect,
will of God.*

Romans 12:2

Faith was nervous at the prospect of the buggy ride.
She liked Ben very much, but he wasn't really much of
a talker and she hoped the conversation would flow
easily and not be stilted, like it had been in the past.

"Are you all right, *Dat?*" Faith noticed her *dat* had
the sick look on his face again—the gray look had
returned.

"I think I need to go to the hospital."

No one could hear what he said. Faith looked at

her *mamm* quickly and saw that deep lines were visible in her forehead.

"What, *Dat?*" Faith leaned in close to hear him.

"Hospital—need to go." His voice was weak.

Faith took in a deep breath. She knew there was something seriously wrong with her *dat* to ask to go to the hospital when he had never even visited a doctor. Faith turned to find someone to take him to the hospital and Ben was the first person she saw.

"Ben, quick; *dat* needs to go to the hospital."

Ben disappeared and moments later pulled up just outside, blasting the car horn. He stepped out of the car and yelled at them. "C'mon, get him in."

Faith felt her mouth fall open. She had never seen Ben in a car and never even knew he could even drive one.

Faith and her *mamm* helped put her *dat* in the front

seat and then they jumped in the back. Ben drove as fast as he could to the hospital. Faith was certain he was driving way over the acceptable speed.

Ben pulled the car up into the hospital's 'emergency only' section for the ambulances. Ben ran into the hospital and came out with two men in white uniforms who were wheeling a bed. They lifted Mr. Fisher on to it.

Ben ducked his head into the car. "You two get out and I'll park the car."

Faith could barely breathe as she walked through the automatic opening doors of the sterile hospital with her *mudder* close by her side.

"What did he say to you back at the restaurant, *Mamm?* Was he in pain anywhere?"

"Nee, I don't know." Her *mamm's* voice was quiet and was more of a whimper.

A lady dressed in white with a fine pinstriped apron came toward them. "I'll need someone to fill out some paperwork for Mr. Fisher." She had a wooden clipboard in her hand with some forms clipped to the top.

Faith took the clipboard and filled out the requested details about her dat. Then she handed the paperwork back when they were directed to a waiting room.

Ben appeared five minutes later and sat in the row of chairs facing them. "Any news?"

Faith just shook her head. She was sure the large lump in her throat would not allow her to speak.

What seemed like two hours later, a man in a white coat asked them to come with him. He directed them into a small, private office and he asked them to sit down. His nametag read, Dr. Waltham.

"What's happening; can we see him?" Faith's *mamm* asked.

"I'm afraid it was too late for us to help him."

Faith's heart froze and she could feel burning behind her eyes. Was the doctor saying what she thought he was saying? Was her father gone? Had this doctor taken them away from the public waiting room into this small office to deliver to them the worst news possible?

Faith noticed her *mamm* straightening her back. "What's wrong with him?"

The doctor looked straight into Mrs. Fisher's eyes. "I'm sorry, we did all we could."

"Has he gone?" her *mamm* asked point blank.

"I'm afraid so. He had a heart attack and there was nothing we could do to save him."

Faith's *mamm* put her head in her hands and

sobbed uncontrollably. Faith put her hand on her *mamm's* back and stroked her.

"I'm sorry," Ben said quietly.

Faith looked at him and nodded appreciatively.

"Would you like to see him?" Dr. Waltham asked.

Mrs. Fisher lifted up her head and with tears in her eyes said, "Nee, it's not him. It's just his body."

Her *mamm's* voice was so small and pitiful that tears flooded down Faith's face. The tears were not only for the fact that she was left without a father; her tears were also for her mother, who was now alone without a *mann* to look after her. Her mother had always seemed so helpless and frail and now she was alone.

Dr. Waltham rose from his chair. "I'll leave you alone for a while. If you have any questions, just ask for me at the reception desk and I'll be back to speak to you."

"Thank you, doctor," Faith said.

The doctor leaned over to Ben and said in a loud whisper, "I'm sorry, but there's paperwork to fill in before you go." Dr. Waltham looked at Faith as her *mamm* had her eyes closed tightly. "If there is anything I can do, please don't hesitate to ask."

"Thank you doctor," Faith said.

Ben nodded.

* * *

Ben drove Faith and her *mamm* home from the hospital. As they approached their home, Faith noticed that it was in pitch darkness and uneasiness filled her body. Someone was always home and she had never seen the house look so alone and empty.

Once they were out of the car, Ben said, "I'll go and get your buggy later and bring it back."

Faith's *mudder* headed to the *haus* from the car, as if in a daze.

Faith whispered to Ben, "*Denke,* Ben. You've been so helpful to us. I appreciate all you've done."

Ben smiled and put his hand out to her. Faith touched his hand softly and tingles went up her arm and circled gently around her neck.

"I'm glad I was there to help." They held each other's gaze for a moment before Ben said, "I'll be back in a while with the buggy."

Faith nodded, then turned and headed toward the *haus.* Faith had no idea what time it was, but she knew it was somewhere in the early hours of the morning.

Mrs. Fisher went straight to bed despite Faith's attempts to have her eat something or at least have a hot lemon tea.

Once Faith was between the warm covers of her own bed, she allowed her mind to be tormented by the events of the day. Her *dat* had gone to be with the Lord on the very same day that her close friend had got married. How strange this world is, she thought. Lilly would not even know that *dat* has gone. Faith had not even asked what her *dat* had passed away from. She was almost certain that the doctor had said it was a heart attack; then again, she could have imagined it because she wasn't thinking straight at the time.

Ben had talked to the doctor for quite a while as he was filling out the last of the paperwork. Faith wondered whether Ben would be back with the buggy tonight; she was too tired to wait up for him. He would just have to put the buggy and the horse away by himself. He would have had another buggy follow him so he could have someone drive him home.

Faith woke very early the next morning with thoughts of how she was going to cope with this life if her *dat* was not in it. She was grateful that she didn't have to work today. Today she would have to let everyone know of her father's passing. Even her four older sisters had no idea yet about their father.

Faith brought her *mamm* breakfast in bed. Her *mamm* sat up a little and made an attempt to eat, then she informed Faith she was going to stay in bed all day and then she would be better.

Faith headed to the barn to hitch the buggy, but saw that the buggy wasn't yet back. *That's unusual; I'm sure he would've had it back by now,* Faith thought. She heard the phone in the barn, but didn't get to it in time to answer. She figured that whoever just called her would have to call back later. She called a taxi and then walked to the end of the drive to wait for it.

There was so much to do: tell the bishop, organize the funeral, tell her sisters and other family, organize the restaurant, and lots of small things, too.

Verity and Reuben were the first people who Faith told. The horse and buggy were still behind the B&B where her *dat* had left them. Faith was surprised that Ben had left them there rather than drive them home as he had said. Faith was pleased to learn that Reuben had looked after the horse and he even offered to take it back to the Fishers later that day. Faith accepted his offer as she had no idea when Ben planned to do it.

No one knew what had become of Ben. According to Ben's parents, who Faith visited later that day, they had not seen him since the wedding.

Verity and her other sisters visited their mother to check on her while Faith continued to tell the community and the bishop about her father.

The bishop was the main person she wanted to speak to. He would be able to tell her what she needed to do to organize the funeral. She had to do as much as she could to take the burden away from her distressed mother.

The taxi left her right outside of Bishop John's front door. The bishop and his wife came out to meet her as if they had been waiting for her.

"I'm sorry to hear about your dat."

"*Denke*. You heard, then?"

"*Jah*, Ben called us."

"*Jah*," his wife added. "Ben called us from jail."

Faith gasped and her hand went to her mouth. "What?"

The bishop glared at his wife for her sudden outburst, and then said to Faith, "He called us early this morning."

"*Jah*, from jail," his wife interrupted.

The bishop ignored his wife and continued. "He told us what happened, and said the car he drove you to the hospital in was borrowed."

"Borrowed? You mean he borrowed it without asking the owner?" Faith could not believe what she heard.

"Exactly. He said he had to get your *dat* to the hospital quickly. He saw the car with the keys in the ignition and he acted quickly." The bishop chuckled slowly. "I've only just got back from talking to the police and the owner of the car. After they found out the circumstances, they aren't pressing charges."

"Is he all right?" Faith was sad that Ben had been to jail over doing her family a nice thing.

"He's fine. Now, do come inside. We need to

speak about some things."

Faith took a deep breath and walked with the bishop into his house. She was pleased that the bishop didn't mind that Ben had driven a car in an emergency, as normally Amish are not supposed to drive at all.

Faith had had too many shocks in a short space of time. She had the death of her father and then the shock of Ben being in jail. She did not think she could cope with any more surprises.

CHAPTER 5

For God so loved the world, that he gave his only begotten Son, that whosoever believeth in him should not perish, but have everlasting life.

John 3:16

There were so many things to organize that Faith's head was spinning. She was grateful that Bishop John and his *fraa* were helping her with so many of the arrangements with the funeral.

Faith was heading home at the end of the long day, and then changed her mind and took a detour to Ben's place. She had to see how he was and thank him for all he had done. As soon as she closed the door of the taxi, she noticed Ben was at his front door.

"Ben, I heard what happened; are you all right?"

Ben laughed. "*Jah,* I'm alright; just a misunderstanding. I'm sorry I haven't got your buggy back yet."

"Misunderstanding? Bishop John told me that you took that car without asking."

"There was no time to ask. I had to get your *vadder* to the hospital."

"*Denke* for doing that for us."

"You're welcome. Most people would do the same."

"Don't worry about the buggy; Reuben is bringing it back today."

"Oh, that's good."

Faith smiled and wondered if most people would do the same. Would it occur to someone to look in a car to see if the keys were left in it? Faith hadn't even known that Ben knew how to drive a car. *I wonder if he even has a driver's license,* she thought.

"Come, sit." Ben nodded his head to the chairs on the porch.

Faith sat down and Ben moved the other chair right next to hers.

"Ben, I need to know what the doctor said to you. We didn't ask what was wrong with dat. He only became sick a few days ago and he didn't seem that bad. We were too upset to ask questions at the hospital."

"As the doctor explained to me, not all heart attacks are accompanied by pains in the chest. He said he may have experienced fatigue, nausea, lack of appetite, or shortness of breath."

"So it was a heart attack," she affirmed to herself. Faith lifted her head and stared into the distance as she recalled his symptoms. *"Jah,* he could've had all of those things, now that I think about it."

"Faith, there was nothing you or your *mudder* could've done. When the Lord wants you home, I think he wants you home, and that's that."

Faith was comforted by Ben's strength, not only his words. He had a real inner strength that Faith knew she was just beginning to discover.

"Faith." Ben's mother came through the door. "I'll be over tomorrow to visit your *mamm.*"

"She'd like that, I'm sure."

Mrs. Schrumb appeared to be studying the two of them before she said, "I'll bring you two some tea and biscuits."

"Okay, *denke, Mamm,*" Ben said.

When Mrs. Schrumb disappeared inside the house, Ben and Faith smiled at each other. It was obvious that Ben's *mamm* was pleased that the two of them were speaking privately. Mrs. Schrumb could have invited her into the *haus* to talk to her as well if she had thought otherwise. Faith was pleased that it seemed as though she met with Ben's *mamm*'s approval.

"So, was it horrible in jail?"

"It wasn't a real jail; it was just at the station where they lock people up overnight. It wasn't nice, though, and I was so glad when I got out."

Faith studied Ben's kind face. He took a risk to help her father and that was something that she would never forget. She hoped that a deep love would develop between the two of them, but if it didn't, she would remain forever in his debt for what he had done to help her *familye. He didn't even think twice about it; he just acted,* Faith thought. *I admire his strength of character, even though it was technically a wrong thing he did when he took that car without asking.*

* * *

Mr. Fisher's funeral

"Faith, I can't have him in the *haus* now. He was once so full of life. His body is no longer him. It's just a shell that he once lived in."

"I understand, *mamm.*" Faith hoped her *mamm* would not suffer any criticism for her decision because the deceased in their Amish community would normally remain in the family home some days before the funeral for friends and family to say good-bye.

Mr. Fisher's body was taken straight from the hospital to the funeral home, and Mrs. Fisher supplied a white shirt and trousers for her husband to be clothed in. She also arranged for the funeral home to do the viewings for anyone who wanted to view him.

The funeral carriage pulled up to the Fisher's

home just before all the guests arrived for the service. All the guests more than filled the Fisher's home to capacity. As they could not all fit into the *haus,* many people were on the porch listening as the bishop gave the service. The bishop's words were surrounding life and death, and touched on how our lives are just a whisper in the moment of time, just a blink of an eye in terms of *Gott's* eternity. Once the bishop's talk was finished, one of the ministers read out a hymn.

Faith sat in front of the bishop with her mother and her four sisters. Her eyes were drawn to the guests standing on the porch and she saw that one of the people standing in the crowd was Lilly. She'd come back from her honeymoon in New York to be at the funeral. Faith closed her eyes and thanked *Gott* for such a friend.

It seemed everyone had come to the funeral. There

was a long procession of gray buggies following the funeral carriage along the driveway and up the main road, which led to the graveside.

Faith was tired from having to make all the arrangements and do all the paperwork required when a person passes. She still had to keep up with all the commitments of the restaurant too. Work was piling onto Faith's shoulders from every direction.

As Faith walked back to the buggy from the graveside, Ben caught up with her. "Is there anything I can do to help you, Faith?"

"*Nee, denke,* Ben. Not that I can think of right now, anyway."

"I would like to see you again soon, when you're ready."

"I'd like that, too."

Having not heard from him for days, she was

worried that Ben had forgotten her, but now she realized that he was just giving her a little space. That knowledge gave her a small piece of comfort. She did not know when she would be ready to see Ben again; there were too many other things on her mind to think about something as frivolous as romance and love.

Only days ago, romance and love seemed to be the only important thing in Faith's life, but now the idea of romance had moved many notches down from first place in her agenda.

CHAPTER 6

Commit thy works unto the Lord, and thy thoughts

shall be established.

Proverbs 16:3

After Faith had finished the late shift at the restaurant, she walked through the front door of her house to see her mother looking worried.

"Faith, I've got some bad news for you." Her mother clutched papers to her chest.

Faith could only assume that the papers were bills, so she hurried to the couch to sit down. "More bad news?" How could she cope with more bad news?

"Just don't tell Verity or Reuben, please?" Her mother sat down next to her and placed the papers in her lap.

Faith took a deep breath and prepared herself for the worst. "*Jah,* okay, what is it?"

"I had the accountant go over the books for the businesses, and it appears that we are in massive debt."

"Massive debt?"

Her mother leafed through the papers in front of her. "*Jah,* those were the exact words of the accountant."

Faith searched her mind to see if she could remember whether her father had ever mentioned such a thing as debts or ever mentioned money issues to her at all. "How can we be in debt? *Dat* never borrowed money."

"That's what I thought, but from the paperwork I found, it appears that he did go to a bank to take a loan a year ago." Her mother held up a paper in her hands.

"Really?" Faith's stomach began to churn.

Mrs. Fisher placed the paper back on top of the pile with the other papers. "*Jah*, he owed a lot of money to the suppliers, and he borrowed money from the bank to pay them all. Then it appears he kept borrowing."

"Kept borrowing?" The words were hard to hear. "That can't be right. The restaurant is doing really well. We're so busy all the time."

Mrs. Fisher nodded. "According to the accountant, the restaurant would've been okay; it's the B&B and all the renovations that have dragged it down."

Faith feared the worst, which was that was that they would become homeless. "Does that mean we have to sell? What would we live on?"

"We can't sell. The accountant said no one would buy a 'lame duck.'"

"A lame duck? That's terrible. Is it that bad?" Faith bit her lip.

Mrs. Fisher's eyes brimmed with tears.

"Mamm, don't cry. It won't help anything. We have to be strong so we can figure this out."

Her mother dried her eyes and dabbed at them with the corner of one of her cotton handkerchiefs.

"That's better." *Everything seems to fall on my shoulders all the time, and I'm the youngest of the family. I had to arrange the funeral, and now I have to bear the burden of this massive debt.* Faith felt very sorry for herself.

"We can't tell anyone, Faith."

Faith inhaled deeply and nodded.

Mrs. Fisher continued, "The accountant said I should go to the bank with all the figures from both businesses and borrow a little more money to tide us over for a while until the B&B starts making some more money."

"Okay, well, that's not so bad." Faith plastered a fake smile on her face.

Faith's mother nodded. "I'll make an appointment to see someone tomorrow."

"Why don't you want Verity to know? Wouldn't it be better if you told her?"

"*Nee,* I can't tell her or Reuben. I don't want to worry anyone and I don't want them to think that I'm going to sell the B&B."

"So, if you sold the B&B, would that get us out of trouble?"

Mrs. Fisher tugged at the corners of her handkerchief. "The accountant said that if we sold the B&B, the business and the building, then our debt would be wiped clean."

Faith put both hands in the air. "So should we do

that? The restaurant makes a lot of money."

"Verity and Reuben would have nowhere to live and now they have the *boppli* and everything. I couldn't leave them homeless."

A large pain was developing in Faith's neck; she knew it was stress. "They could live here or with Reuben's parents."

"*Nee,* I could not do that to them. Reuben's put so much work into the renovations and Verity's done so much work, as well."

Faith nodded; she knew how much work they had both done to the place. She also knew they would both be devastated if the place had to be sold. What if everything had to be sold, though? "What if we lose everything by trying to keep the B&B? Wouldn't it be better just to sell the B&B and at least we'd have the income from the restaurant to live on?"

Faith's mother's eye's glazed over as she looked at her *dochder*. "I don't know, Faith. I just don't know."

Faith knew that the general economy in Lancaster County and the whole country was quite bad, with many people being fired from their jobs and others unable to find work. The tourist community kept the restaurants and shops in Lancaster doing quite well; however, the restaurants and B&Bs had to be very competitive to earn the tourist dollar.

"Do you want me to come with you when you go to the bank?"

"*Jah,* that would be *gut, denke.* I don't understand a lot of these things; your *dat* always looked after the finances."

"What made you have the accountant go over the books?"

"I had trouble getting money from your *vadder's*

account for the funeral. His account was joined to the business accounts. I had to use some money I had in a personal account. I knew straight away that something wasn't right."

* * *

Mrs. Fisher had made an appointment with the same bank where they already had a loan. She was hoping they would at least increase the loan temporarily. Once they arrived at the bank, they were shown to a small waiting room where they sat in emerald-green leather chairs. Faith could tell her mother was very nervous, as her fingers kept fiddling with the corners of the paperwork on her lap.

When the bank clerk called out the name of Mrs. Fisher, Faith followed her mother to a small cubicle.

In the cubicle, they were faced with a small, bald gentleman who looked to be in his sixties, who was hiding behind a large computer screen.

"Have a seat," he said, as he momentarily glanced up before he returned to tap away at his computer keyboard.

Once they were both seated in front of the loan manager's desk, he gave them his full attention. "Now, what can I do for you?"

"We have a loan with your bank already …" Her mother was interrupted.

"Just a moment." He tapped some things into his computer. "Yes, I see. I also see that your loan is in default."

"It is?" Faith was pretty sure that meant they were behind in their loan and that was not a good thing.

"By $2,089.26." The loan manager looked away

from his computer, clasped his hands together on the desk, and looked between Faith and her mother. "If the loan isn't brought up to date, you could face serious penalties and be put into the hands of debt collectors."

Faith looked at her mother, hoping she would say something. Did they even have $2,000.00 they could put toward the loan? Would the bank loan them more money if they couldn't even keep up the payments with their current loan?

Mrs. Fisher straightened in her chair, looked directly at the loan manager, and said, "We're here in the hope that you'll be able to loan us more money."

Faith wanted to sink into her chair or become invisible. Even she knew that they were about to be tossed out of the bank. *Oh, Gott, please help us*, she prayed silently.

The small old man leaned back in his chair. "How do you propose to pay back the money? This loan is already in default. Do you have the money with you to bring this loan up to date?"

"Not on me right now, but I can get it," Mrs. Fisher insisted.

Faith was proud of her mother. She doubted that she had the money to bring the loan up to date, but she did sound very convincing.

"I've brought these income figures from my accountant." Mrs. Fisher handed over a bundle of papers.

After a few moments of looking over the paperwork, the loan manager said, "The income looks good, but your outgoings seem abnormally high. Then there's the current loan to take into account, as well." He passed the papers back. "I'm sorry, but on these figures and with the current loan, we just can't lend you any more money."

"We're going through a rough patch at the moment, but we'll come good. My husband has only just died and we need a little help. Can you give us a little more time?"

The loan manager leaned forward. "Mrs. Fisher, what do you think would come of the bank if we just loaned money to people willy nilly? The bank has to make a profit. We've got shareholders. The bank is a business like any other business. We can only loan money to people if we know that we will be paid back. From the looks of your figures, it doesn't appear that you will be able to do that. I'm sorry about your husband, but there's nothing I can do. The figures speak for themselves."

"Well, what do you suggest we do, then?"

"You need to get your loan up to date, or you'll end up paying a lot of interest and possibly face a high fine if it goes on for too long like this. As I said before, a debt collection service may take over the loan if it gets any further overdue." He leaned back in his chair. "That's how things stand." He gave a quick nod of his head, almost as if he were dismissing them.

Mrs. Fisher jutted out her chin at the man. "Well, if we have to go bankrupt, you won't get any of your money back. So wouldn't it be better for the bank if they helped us now?"

The man leaned forward and raised his voice. "If you don't bring the loan up to date, we can increase our charges, put it in the hands of debt collectors, and I should tell you that we are also able to bring criminal charges against you."

Mrs. Fisher gasped at his threats and his rude

manner. "You don't need to be so rude. We came here just asking for a little help and a little extra time, that's all."

Faith could see that things were going nowhere. It was plain to see that this bank would certainly not loan them any money whatsoever. "C'mon, *mamm.*"

As they walked out of the bank, Faith whispered, "Why don't we try another bank?"

"I don't know. I need to think about things for a while." Her mother's tone was full of defeat.

"Did the accountant say why the outgoings are so high?"

"I'm not sure. I'll have a look at them tomorrow. I just want to go home."

Faith knew her mother was feeling quite depressed. So was Faith after speaking to the man at the bank. He was unnecessarily rude and overbearing for such a small, insignificant looking man.

CHAPTER 7

If we confess our sins, he is faithful and just to forgive

us our sins, and to cleanse us from all unrighteousness.

1 John 1:9

Faith was annoyed with her mother for forbidding her to tell Reuben of their situation. He would have been the perfect person with which to discuss business matters. He had gone to New York and made millions of dollars in a short space of time before he returned to Verity and to the Amish. He would know about balance sheets, loans, and outgoings. Yet her hands were tied, as she promised her mother she would not tell Reuben or Verity, about their financial predicament.

* * *

Faith usually took the late shift at the restaurant, but today she was working the early shift. Mrs. Fisher had insisted on coming in with her to oversee the operations of the restaurant.

Just before Faith unlocked the front door of the restaurant, her mother said, "Faith, I have a meeting with a man who I think will loan us some money."

"Which bank is he from?"

"No bank. He has a lot of money and he loans it to people. Like a bank, except he is a person with a lot of money."

"Oh." Faith had heard about private lenders and she knew that their interest rates were extraordinarily high. "How high is the interest?"

Her mother shrugged her shoulders and hugged

the paperwork in her hands, close to her chest. "I'm not sure. That's what the meeting is about."

"Have you met him before?" Faith was uneasy about the situation. If only her father were still alive, he would know what to do. Her mother had never been involved in business of any kind before. Sure, she owned the restaurant and the B&B with her late husband, but she had never taken an active role in the running of either of them.

"I spoke to him over the phone. It was funny how it happened; I prayed and then straight away my eyes fell to a newspaper that Reuben had in the B&B and the advertisement was right there before my eyes. I'm meeting him here at three p.m. today."

Faith hoped that this man had been sent by *Gott* to help them. "Oh, good. I'll be here then. Mind if I sit in?" Faith knew the best option would have been to tell Reuben and let him take over the business side of things, but she knew her mother would not hear of it. She would just have to help the best that she could.

Her mother put her hand gently on Faith's shoulder and gave a little smile. "I was hoping you would."

Faith had not seen her mother smile very much since her father had gone to be with the Lord. "So, what did the advertisement say exactly?"

"Along the lines of—*can't get a loan from a bank? Richard Black, private lender of finance.*"

* * *

At exactly three p.m., Richard Black walked through the double glass doors of the restaurant. Faith knew who he was straight away, as he had a self-important air about him, as Faith imagined one would have if they had a lot of money. Faith considered he could easily be the tallest man she had ever seen. He had close shaven, dark brown hair, a solid build, and eyes that were hiding behind a pair of what Faith could only assume were costly designer sunglasses.

Faith made sure she approached him before the other waitress who was working that day.

"Are you looking for Mrs. Fisher?" Apart from his sunglasses and a flashy gold watch, he wasn't dressed in expensive looking clothes. *I suppose with that much money, he doesn't have to impress anyone*, Faith thought. *Then again, the watch and the sunglasses would most likely impress people.* He wore casual, cream-colored pants and a white shirt, which had one too many buttons undone to reveal a tanned chest. He held a large, black folder. Faith noticed his hands had never seen a day's labor.

They appeared to be soft, and his nails were manicured. As he smiled at Faith, she noticed that his perfect shaped teeth were unnaturally white. Faith considered him to be in his mid forties.

"Yes, I'm Richard Black, here to see Mrs. Fisher. Is she here yet?"

"This way."

Richard Black followed Faith to a table in the back of the restaurant, where they would be able to speak uninterrupted.

When he sat down, Faith said, "Mrs. Fisher is my mother and I'm Faith." Faith put her hand out to shake Mr. Black's hand. Then she said, "I'll go and tell her you're here." *I was right; his hands have never seen a day's work, soft like a boppli's bottom.*

"Thank you." Mr. Black placed the black book on the table in front of him.

"*Mamm*, he's here."

Her mother had been waiting in the small staff room. She stood up and took a couple of deep breaths. "Okay. I'm ready."

"He's at the corner table." Faith followed her mother out to Richard Black.

The next thing Faith saw, she could hardly believe. The look on Richard Black's face when he saw her mother come walking toward him was something that Faith had seldom seen. Richard Black immediately stood to his feet and accidently knocked over the chair next to him. He didn't even notice the chair, though, as his eyes were transfixed on her mother.

Oh, he's attracted to mamm, Faith realized. Faith had never thought of her mother attracting a man. It was then that Faith realized that her mother was a beautiful woman, even though she had five children and even though she had been married for close to twenty-five years to one man. *I think mamm's forty-seven and this mann might be around the same age,* she considered.

Faith had no idea whether or not her mother noticed this man's attraction toward her. Once her mother and Richard were seated, Faith approached the table. "Do you mind if I sit in?"

"Please do." Richard smiled at her.

Before Faith sat, she asked, "Would you like something to drink, coffee or anything?"

"I'd like an herbal tea of some sort if you have it."

"Sure." Faith turned her head to her mother. "And you?"

"I'm fine, *denke.*" Faith could tell by the sound of her mother's voice that she was nervous.

Faith picked up the knocked over chair and then raced to get Richard a cup of herbal tea and returned to the table. "What have I missed?"

"Nothing, we were waiting for you to return," Richard said. "So, you need to borrow some money?"

"Yes, we need to borrow $50,000.00 and the bank won't lend us the money." Her mother bit her lip. Faith knew she was wondering if she should have told him that the bank wouldn't loan them the money.

As if sensing her concern, Richard said, "Don't worry, if the bank loaned everyone money, I wouldn't have any customers." He gave a little chuckle and Faith considered that he was trying to put them at ease. Richard nodded to the paperwork in Mrs. Fisher's hands. "Is that for me to look at?"

"I guess so. The bank wanted to see the figures so I thought you would too. I'm not sure how these things work."

Richard took the paperwork and began to sift

through it. Every now and again he took a sip of his herbal tea.

While he looked at the paperwork, Faith tried hard not to look at his face, but she couldn't help it. Faith could tell he was aged somewhere in his forties yet he hardly had a wrinkle on his face except for some tiny lines at the corners of his eyes. She couldn't help but wonder if he'd had some sort of cosmetic surgery. Faith also wondered whether her mother thought that Richard was a handsome man.

Faith glanced at her mother and noticed that she would have been too nervous to notice whether this man was handsome or not.

"Hmm, and how much did you borrow from the bank and when did you borrow it?" Richard asked.

"You see," Faith began, "My father passed away recently; he borrowed the money about a year ago."

Richard Black moved uncomfortably in his seat and looked at Mrs. Fisher. "I'm so sorry to hear that."

Mrs. Fisher closed her lips tightly together and her eyes misted over as if she was about to cry. She nodded in response to Richard's sympathy.

He directed his next question to Faith. "What was the loan amount?"

"I am pretty sure it was $150,000.00" Faith swallowed hard and found it hard to take her next breath. She was sure it was closer to $200,000.00 and she had just told a big, fat fib. What else could she do? Her family's livelihood was at stake and so was Verity's family's livelihood.

"And the interest rate?" Faith shrugged her shoulders and looked at her mother

Richard also looked at Mrs. Fisher. "I think it was eight point something percent."

"Secured or unsecured?"

Mrs. Fisher shook her head and tears welled up in her eyes. Faith froze in her seat, not knowing what she should do. Her natural instinct was to comfort her mother, but they needed this money and she didn't want Richard Black to think they were total weaklings who let their emotions run their business.

"Secured—I think." Faith blurted out her answer without thinking. She had no idea what either term meant or whether she had said the right thing.

"I see." Mr. Black's eyes flickered quickly between the two women in front of him.

By the look on Mr. Black's face, Faith perceived that he knew that neither she nor her mother knew what they were talking about in regards to loans and finance. It was clear to Faith that this high-powered lending machine of a man would definitely not loan them any money.

"Who runs the businesses?"

"Well, my father used to run this business. Now that he's gone, mother runs it. My sister and her husband run the B&B."

Mr. Black placed his large hand on the pages in front of him, once again. "I can see that the income from the B&B is steadily increasing."

"Yes, Reuben, my sister's husband, is very good at business." Faith knew that Reuben's business sense was one positive thing in their favor, but not if her mother refused to let him know of their dire situation.

"Reuben King?" Mr. Black's eyes grew wide.

"Yes, do you know him?"

"Not personally, but from what I've heard of him, I'd say the B&B would be in good hands." Mr. Black clasped his hands in front of his face, placing his elbows on the table. "$50,000.00 is a lot of money. I usually charge fourteen percent." He dug his chin into his knuckles. "I'll tell you what I'm prepared to do. I will loan you $50,000 over a five-year period, and match the interest rate of the bank."

Faith and her mother exchanged excited glances.

"But … I want to personally watch over these finances." He held the papers in the air. "I'd like to help the two of you make a real success of this business. It looks like things have really slipped in the past couple of years. Someone took their eye off the ball. Your outgoings are way too high. I'd like to look into them, if I might."

"Oh, yes. Thank you so much. We'd be delighted if you'd do that. Wouldn't we, *mamm?*" Faith looked at her *mamm,* who was sitting rigidly and fighting back tears.

Finally, her mother spoke. "Thank you so much, Mr. Black. It's so kind of you to offer to help us in so many ways."

Mr. Black stared intently at Mrs. Fisher. It was obvious to Faith that Mr. Black was quite taken with her mother. Her complexion was pale and flawless; not a gray hair was to be seen on the dark red hair that was visible at the front of her prayer *kapp*. Faith was convinced that Mr. Black was attracted to her mother and that was the only reason he was being extra helpful.

It was very kind of the mysterious Richard Black to offer them the money and help in the business, but Faith couldn't shake the feeling that they had just jumped out of the frying pan and into the fire.

CHAPTER 8

If we confess our sins, he is faithful and just to forgive

us our sins, and to cleanse us from all unrighteousness.

Romans 5:8

It was unusual for Faith's mother to be up early since her husband had passed. Usually she didn't get out of bed until much later in the day, but today, the sound of rattling around in the kitchen reached Faith before Faith had even gotten out of bed.

Faith staggered to the kitchen. *"Mamm,* what are you doing awake so early?"

Her mother's hair hadn't even been brushed; she had no prayer *kapp* on and she was in her nightdress. "Cooking you breakfast before you have to go to work, that's what."

Faith sat at the dining table, which was already prepared for breakfast. "You must be feeling a little better."

"*Jah,* I am feeling better. It was *Gott's* will to take your *vadder,* so I have to accept that and get on with things."

Faith nodded and wondered why *Gott* had decided to take her father so early, before he was very old. Especially since it put them in a complete mess with the businesses.

"Faith, I have someone very special coming for dinner tonight. Can you have someone cover your shift starting at five o'clock?"

"I suppose I can see if I can have someone work back. Someone's always looking for some overtime work. Why, who's coming to dinner?" Faith was a little worried that overtime work meant overtime pay, but her mother seemed quite oblivious to that fact.

Her mother giggled and turned back to the eggs that were cooking on the stove. "It's a surprise."

"Look at me, *Mamm.*"

Mrs. Fisher turned to face her and Faith searched her face.

"That's not fair; you have to tell me."

Mrs. Fisher lifted the pan off the stove and served the eggs onto two plates. *"Nee,* I do not have to tell you."

"Will I be pleased about it?"

"Jah, I think you will be very pleased to see who I have invited."

Faith wondered if her mother knew that Faith liked Ben. Maybe her mother did notice the way they interacted at Lilly's wedding. *Mamm would be very grateful to Ben for getting dat to the hospital so quickly.*

Mrs. Fisher placed the two plates of eggs on the table and sat down opposite Faith.

After playing with her poached eggs, Faith lifted a forkful to her mouth. "All right, don't tell me, then. I think I know anyway." Faith popped the egg into her mouth.

"I don't think you do."

"Don't do this to me, *Mamm.*" Faith groaned, which caused her mother to giggle. "Are you trying to match me up with someone?"

Mrs. Fisher shrugged her shoulders. "Maybe, maybe not."

Faith shook her head and gave up trying to get a straight answer. She hoped again her mother had invited Ben for dinner. If it was anyone other than Ben, Faith decided that she would not be happy about it.

"Are you coming into work today?" Faith hoped that her mother would take more of an interest in the business and gain more of an understanding of how things ran. Faith did not want all the responsibilities of the business on her shoulders. It seemed to Faith that was exactly what was happening.

"Jah, Richard wants to go over some paperwork with me."

"Has he seen our accountant?"

"I suggested he should talk to Mr. Benny, but he made a comment about him not being a very efficient accountant."

Faith raised her eyebrows. She did not know whom to trust. Mr. Benny had been their accountant for years, but their business had gotten into serious trouble while he was looking after the finances. Was that Mr. Benny's fault or was that her father's fault?

Faith had no idea. "So, what do you think about Mr. Benny?"

"I have no idea. No idea." Her mother's voice was more of a whimper.

Faith tried to change the subject slightly to try and keep her mother from dwelling on anything negative. "So, is it Mr. Black who's coming to dinner?"

Mrs. Fisher's lips turned upward at the corners. "*Nee*, he's not coming to dinner. Someone like that would not want to have dinner with people like us."

Nee, but he might want to have dinner with you, though, Faith thought. It was clear to Faith that her mother still had no idea that Richard Black was attracted to her.

CHAPTER 9

And the peace of God, which passeth all understanding, shall keep your hearts and minds through Christ Jesus.

Philippians 4:7

Faith was getting home late; she was disappointed to see that the buggy in front of the house was definitely not Ben's buggy. Ben's horse was a tall bay, whereas this one was black all over with one white sock. Faith was sure that she wouldn't know whoever was inside unless they had just purchased a new horse. A flame of anger rose within her. *After all the stress I've been through lately, now mamm is trying to match me up with someone, who from the looks of the buggy, I don't even know.*

As Faith walked through the front door, her eyes

fell on Jakob Lapp, who was sitting on the couch in the living room. Faith recalled that Jakob had two daughters, who Faith figured were around ten or twelve, and he had been a widower for around three years.

"Hello, Jakob, isn't it?"

Jakob rose to his feet. *"Jah,* nice to see you again."

Faith's *familye* had never really been close to the Lapp *familye*. Faith knew that Jakob's mother was a meddling old gossip of a woman, but Faith couldn't hold that against the woman's son.

"I last saw you at your *vadder's* funeral."

Faith nodded and sat down on a chair opposite him. *"Jah,* that's right."

"He's in a better place now."

Faith smiled, yet she could not help the annoyance that rose within her whenever people said that her father was in 'a better place' or that it was 'his time to go.' She wanted him there with her, not in heaven and not with the Lord. Surely her father would want to be here with his family for a few more years. She tried to hide her annoyance; the man in front of her was only being polite.

Mrs. Fisher came in from the kitchen. "Here you are."

"*Jah,* sorry I'm late. Do you want some help with anything?" Faith stood up.

"*Nee,* you sit down. Everything is under control and dinner will be ready in twenty minutes."

Faith sat down and was upset when her mother disappeared back to the kitchen, leaving her to speak to the much older Jakob. It was only after her mother was in the kitchen that she realized this was her mother's plan to save the restaurant and the B&B. It was well known that Jakob was a wealthy man and he would never let his would-be *fraa's* family businesses go broke. *So that's mamm's plan, marry me into money.*

Faith not only felt sorry for herself, she felt sorry for Jakob. There was no way she would ever marry an older man like Jakob, even if she wasn't in love with Ben. Jakob was plainly too old for her.

"So, how are your *kinner?*"

"Fine, fine. Lizzy is ten now and Tracey is eleven."

Faith nodded and tried to look interested. "Oh, they've grown up quickly. Who's looking after them tonight?"

"My *mamm* is watching them."

Oh, yes, the crotchety old Mrs. Lapp; I bet the children aren't happy about that, Faith thought.

"She adores the girls."

"Jah, I'm sure she does." Faith had absolutely no

idea what to say to this man. She wished her mother would come back from the kitchen to rescue the forced conversation.

"How do you like working in the restaurant?" He asked.

"I love it; it's lively and busy and the people I work with are great."

If I were older I would think that Jakob is handsome, Faith considered. His bone structure was good, his eyes were a bright blue-green, and his smile was engaging. His reputation was that he was a *gut mann* of *Gott* and a hard worker. *He's closer to mamm's age than mine.*

"Knock, knock."

Faith jumped to her feet. She knew that familiar voice. "Lilly, Jason," she squealed, and ran to open the front door. "Come in."

Jakob stood to his feet.

"Lilly, do you know Jakob?"

"*Jah*, hello Jakob. This is Jason, my new husband."

After the introductions were over, Faith's mother came scurrying out of the kitchen. "Lilly! Hello, Jason. You must stay for dinner."

Lilly looked at Jason, who shrugged his shoulders. "*Denke*, Mrs. Fisher, that would be lovely."

"Sit, sit. Dinner is just minutes away."

Lilly had not been shunned when she left the Amish, as she had not been baptized into the Faith. Her old friends could have limited communication with her.

"I'll come and help you, *Mamm.*" Faith hurried to the kitchen, leaving the three guests in the living room.

"*Mamm,* what do you mean by trying to match me up with Jakob?"

"Hush, or he'll hear you. He'd make you a fine husband."

"I'm not in love with him, and not only that, I hardly know him. He has children; what do I know about children?"

"You'll have your own soon enough when you get married. There's really nothing to it."

Faith rolled her eyes. There was no point even speaking to her mother. Her mother always had an answer for everything. Faith was very grateful that Lilly and Jason had arrived and saved the day. Otherwise, it would have been a very awkward and very long dinner, indeed.

Lilly walked into the kitchen. "Can I help, Mrs. Fisher?"

"*Nee*, Lilly. Oh, well, I suppose you two girls can make the gravy while I go and speak to Jakob and

Jason."

"We can do that," Lilly said.

As soon as Faith's mother was out of the kitchen, Lilly said to Faith, "What's Jakob doing here?"

"*Mamm's* trying to match me up with him, I'd say." Faith opened the oven and a wave of heat flowed over her from the chicken and vegetables that were roasting.

"He's so old. Didn't you tell her that you like Ben?"

Faith closed the oven and checked on the greens that were boiling on the stove. "*Nee*, I guess I should have. Maybe it wouldn't have made a difference."

"Why do you say that?"

"It appears she wants to marry me off to someone rich."

"Why would she? Anyway, Ben's not exactly poor.

He'll inherit the *familye* farm one day, being the eldest boy."

Faith sighed, and then quietly said, "Don't say anything to anyone, but the restaurant's in financial trouble. It seems *mamm* thinks that my marrying Jakob will be the answer to the money problems."

"Oh, I didn't know. How bad are things?"

"Bad enough, but please don't tell anyone." Faith peeped through to the lounge room at her mother talking to Jakob and Jason. "Bad enough for her to want to marry me off to someone I don't even know."

"You simply can't do it. Anyway, Ben likes you."

"Did he say so?" Faith stood to attention as her heart beat faster.

"Not in so many words, but I can tell he likes you." Lilly moved closer to Faith and said in a low voice, "He wouldn't tell me who he likes anyway, but I can tell."

Faith exhaled deeply. "I hope so. Now, how are we going to make this gravy?"

"From the pan juices. Take the chicken and vegetables out of the baking tray, put the baking tray on the top plate, add flour and water, then stir."

"Oh, that's right." Faith followed Lilly's directions for gravy making, while Lilly supervised.

As it turned out, Faith was seated opposite Jakob during dinner. While he talked to her mother, she couldn't help but notice that there were gray hairs amidst his dark hairs at his temples. *What is mamm thinking? I'm not yet twenty and she's trying to marry me off to someone who has gray hair. If it wasn't so tragic, I would laugh at the situation. I feel sorry for Jakob, but whatever is he thinking? Surely he would have to realize what my mamm is up to. Anyway, by the way they are talking to each other, it appears that mamm has far more in common with him than I do. Maybe she should marry him.*

After a lull in the conversation, Faith's mother said, "Very nice gravy, girls."

"You can thank Lilly for that. She instructed me on how to make it."

Lilly laughed. "It's just gravy; it's not difficult."

Jason was seated in between Jakob and his wife, Lilly. He turned to Jakob and said, "It seems all the Amish women are good cooks. Would that be a fair statement, Jakob?"

"Jah, Amish women sure can cook. They are well instructed in cooking from a young age. Recipes are passed down through the generations."

Faith was a little uncomfortable with Jason's question and hoped that Jakob wasn't sadly thinking of his late *fraa* and her cooking.

112

"My girls can already cook at ten and eleven."

"Really? Do they cook for you all the time?" Jason seemed to be truly amazed at the thought of girls that young being proficient at cooking.

"*Jah*, they do it all. Sometimes they might need help with something heavy or cutting up something that's a bit hard."

Jason pulled a face and said, "That's remarkable. It certainly is a different lifestyle to the one I was brought up in. I was a bit of a tear away when I was younger and when I was ten or eleven, I'm sure I sat in front of video games all the time—either that or the television."

Jakob raised his eyebrows, which formed deep lines in his forehead. "What of chores?"

Jason turned his eyes to the ceiling. "I think I had to take out the trash at one point. I never did it, though, so my parents gave up trying to get me to do anything." Jason chuckled.

Jakob shook his head. "Oh, that's bad."

Faith interrupted. "It is?"

"*Jah*, young children need responsibility so they can feel a sense of belonging and being part of the *familye.*"

Faith stared at her mother and said, "That's a point; I never would have known that." Faith's stare was trying to convey to her *mamm*, 'See, I told you I would not make a *gut mudder* to his *kinner!*'

Faith's mother looked away from her daughter as if she had not noticed Faith's pointed comment and her glaring eyes.

Jason said, "I can see that the Amish do have a strong sense of family and a strong sense of belonging to a larger family, which is the community."

"That's right; the community is an excellent place to bring up children. They're protected and looked after, aren't they, Jakob?" Lilly looked at Jakob.

"*Jah*, I would not want to be bringing up *kinner* in the *Englisch* world. There seems to be no respect and no sense of what is right or wrong—not even a sense of what is decent."

Faith looked at Lilly and they gave each other a quick smile. Faith knew that Lilly wanted to bring up her children in the Amish community so was taking advantage of any opportunity to sing the praises of child rearing in the community.

Jakob turned to Jason. "When my wife, Janet, went to be with the Lord, the girls were only around five and six and I had no lack of people offering to help me. I don't know what I would have done without all the help and support I got during that time. The

Amish are just one big *familye;* we support each other."

Jason nodded his head at Jakob's words and kept quiet.

CHAPTER 10

*But they that wait upon the Lord shall renew their
strength; they shall mount up with wings as eagles;
they shall run, and not be weary; and they shall walk,
and not faint.*

Isaiah 40:31

After an enjoyable dinner, Faith had to admit that
Jakob was a very nice man. But he was a very nice man
for someone else, not for her.

Faith and her mother waved goodbye to the two
buggies, then Mrs. Fisher turned to her *dochder.* "Well,
what do you think?"

"About what?"

Mrs. Fisher led Faith out of the cold outside air
and back into the warmth of the *haus* and closed the

door. "About Jakob."

"He seems very nice and I feel very sorry for him that his wife, Janet, died."

"So, you think he is nice?" Faith's mother smiled widely and Faith was sure that her *mamm's* eyes were even twinkling.

"Not for me, though. He's far too old and he's got old children. I can't replace their mother. Besides, I don't know anything about how to care for children of that age."

"You could do far worse. He's a *gut mann* and he's very wealthy. You would not want for anything ever again if you married him."

"Since when do you care about money?" Faith immediately bit her lip, as she knew that money problems were on the forefront of her mother's mind right now.

"We need money to live and to eat. Since your *vadder* died, all this has fallen to me to look after. Your sisters are all married, but what is to become of you? Who will look after you?"

"*Mamm*, I'm only young. I'll get married soon; don't worry about me. Besides, I can look after myself." Faith wondered if that were true. If the restaurant closed down, she had no idea whether it would be easy or not for her to get another job.

"It's not only you; it's all the people who work in the restaurant, as well as Verity and Reuben."

"Everything will work out how it's supposed to; stop worrying. The Scripture says to cast all your burden on Him for He cares for you."

Her mother nodded and pinched her lips tightly together. "*Jah.*"

Faith began to clear the plates from the table.

"Now, I'll clean up and you go to bed."

"All right, *denke.*"

Faith kissed her mother on the cheek and headed to the kitchen, glad to have some time to herself for the first time that day.

So much drama had showed up in her life as soon as her father had passed. He was the person she usually turned to in times of trouble and now he was gone. *Maybe Gott is showing me that I should rely on Him,* she thought, as she scraped the food off the plates and into the rubbish bin.

* * *

It was the second Sunday where there was no meeting and Lilly had invited Faith to her house. Lilly had arranged for Ben to pick up Faith in his buggy. As

Faith waited for Ben to fetch her, she couldn't help but think, *It's not a date if Lilly asked him to pick me up. I wish he had asked me to go somewhere with him.*

From her lounge room, Faith heard the clip clop of the buggy before she saw it. "Bye, *mamm.*"

"Bye," her mother called from the kitchen.

Faith opened the front door and was pleased when she saw Ben's smiling face.

"Hello, Faith. It's a lovely day."

Faith giggled. "It's very cold."

"Jah, I love the cold weather."

Faith climbed into the buggy and Ben handed her a warm, hand-knitted blanket. *"Denke."* Faith didn't know why, but she always felt calm around Ben.

After Ben clicked his horse forward, he asked, "How's your *mudder?"*

"She's getting a little better every day." Faith pulled the blanket up around her neck as the cold wind whistled in from somewhere in the buggy.

Ben glanced at Faith and gave a little smile. Faith looked straight ahead as if she did not notice.

"Have you been to Lilly and Jason's *haus* before?"

"Jah, I helped them move things in. Jason had quite a bit of furniture and things he had to move from his old place."

"Your folks seem okay with Lilly marrying Jason. Seeing that he's not Amish and everything."

"Jah, they would prefer an Amish *mann,* but they have no say really, do they?"

"Jah, I think they would have had quite a bit of influence over Lilly if they had told her they didn't approve. They could have refused to go to the wedding."

Ben looked over at her and smiled. "Is that what you would do if it were your *dochder* marrying an *Englischer?*"

Faith realized that her conversation was far too serious. She drew in a deep breath and let it out slowly. "Hmm, I would not be happy about it, that's for sure and for certain, but I would accept her decision since she is an adult and old enough to make her choice."

"That's what my folks have done."

Faith threw his own question back at him. "Is that what you would've done if it were your *dochder?*" Faith stared at Ben until he looked at her.

"I would have put my foot down and said that *Gott* would not want any *dochder* of mine to marry an *Englischer.* There are plenty of Amish *menner.* She just had to wait a little longer and she would have met one she liked."

Faith could feel her eyebrows rise nearly to her hairline. She had not expected such a definite response from the normally quiet and shy Ben.

"Does that shock you?" Ben asked.

"It does." Faith giggled. "I didn't know you had such a strong opinion."

"The Bible says that the believer should not be unequally yoked with an unbeliever."

"Well, Lilly says that Jason does believe in *Gott*, so he's not really an unbeliever."

"*Jah*, but he doesn't believe as we do, so it's hardly the same."

"I had no idea you thought that way."

"Do my words surprise you?"

"*Jah*, you're normally so quiet."

"I'm not quiet at all; if I have something to say, I'll say it. People only think I'm quiet because I don't prattle on with useless words."

"So you save your words, like they're precious."

Ben looked at Faith and his serious face broke into a smile. "Now, you're teasing me."

"I guess I am." Faith laughed.

"Here we are." Ben drove the buggy up a long driveway and behind a large, two level-white house. The house was on a very large, grassy piece of land, but there was no garden.

Lilly and Jason came out of the back door to greet them.

"Hello, you two," Lilly said.

"I didn't realize you lived this close," Faith said, as she got out of the buggy.

"*Jah*, it's quite close." Lilly linked her arm through Faith's and took her inside the *haus*, leaving the two men alone outside.

"It's such a big *haus,* Lilly."

"We're only here for six months while we save up for a deposit for a home of our own."

The burden and pressure of the restaurant's finances were suddenly evident on Faith's shoulders once more. Lilly had taken two weeks off for her honeymoon and was due back at work the very next day. Lilly was relying on her job at the restaurant to save money for a home. So many other people were relying on the money from their jobs at the restaurant, as well. Her own *schweschder,* Verity, and her *bruder-*in-law were living at the B&B and running it, so it was more than their livelihood; it was also their home. Faith let out a breath slowly and tried to relax her shoulders that had become tight with tension and worry.

"Faith, are you all right?"

Faith brought her mind back to the present moment. "Just thinking that you're coming back to work tomorrow, aren't you?"

"Jah, I've missed working. It was nice to have a break, though."

Lilly walked with Faith into the kitchen.

"Let's have some hot tea." Lilly pulled a dining chair out for Faith to sit in.

Faith sat down, wondering when Ben would come inside. "That sounds lovely. I'll have some lemon tea, if you have it."

"Jah, of course. We've only got an easy lunch today if that's okay."

"It smells delicious. What is it?"

"Split pea and ham soup." Lilly busied herself making the tea. "You know, Jason likes to cook."

Faith giggled and swiveled in her chair to face

Lilly. "Did he cook the soup?"

"*Jah*, he did, and it's quite tasty, too."

At that moment, Ben and Jason came through the door and they sat down at the kitchen table as well.

"So, what have you two ladies been talking about?" Jason asked.

"We've been talking about your cooking." Faith laughed.

Jason smiled. "Well, I've lived by myself for a long time and I had to learn to cook or starve."

"That's unusual for a man to cook," Ben said.

"Not with us *Englischers,* Ben."

Lilly placed a mug of hot tea in front of everyone and sat down.

Jason looked at Ben and then at Faith and said, "So, how long have you two been seeing each other? Or do you call it dating?"

Faith shook her head. "We're not." She noticed that Lilly did not look very happy with Jason's question.

Ben cleared his throat. "Not yet."

Jason threw back his head and laughed. "I've put my foot in it again. I'm quite well known for that. I always open my big mouth."

"*Jah,* you do," Lilly said, and playfully hit him on the back of his shoulder.

Faith glanced across at Ben and smiled and he smiled back.

After they had their fill of soup and hot bread, followed by cheesecake, Ben drove Faith home.

"I hope you weren't embarrassed, Faith. With Jason's question."

"*Nee,* I thought it was funny." Faith cuddled into the warm blanket, and wished that she were cuddling

129

with Ben instead.

"Not too funny, I hope." Ben's brow furrowed.

"I don't mean it like that. I mean that it was a funny situation."

After a few moments, Ben said, "I would like to see a little more of you, Faith."

"I'd like that, too."

Minutes later, Faith was home, watching Ben's buggy disappear up the road. She was frustrated that she had told Ben she would like to see more of him, but he had not made any arrangements to do so. *Sometimes I wish he wasn't so shy. It's very hard to see that he likes me,* she thought.

CHAPTER 11

There hath no temptation taken you but such as is common to man: but God is faithful, who will not suffer you to be tempted above that ye are able; but will with the temptation also make a way to escape, that ye may be able to bear it.

1 Corinthians 10:13

As planned, Richard Black, the man whom they had privately arranged a loan with, arrived to go over the finances with Faith and her mother.

Faith caught his eye as he walked through the door. "Hello," she said. "Just go to the same table as we were at the other day and we'll be with you in a minute."

Richard nodded his head and walked to the table

131

at the back of the restaurant.

Faith pulled Lilly aside. "Lilly, I've just got a meeting with that man over there and *mamm.*"

"Sure, take as long as you like."

Faith looked around. "Oh, bother, I'll have to go and find her; she was here a moment ago."

"Try the B&B. I saw her heading out there a few minutes ago," Lilly said.

"Okay, can you go over there and see if that man would like anything to drink or eat? Tell him we'll just be a few moments."

"Sure."

Faith headed out the back door. She did not like to be late for appointments and she was sure that Richard Black would certainly not like to be kept waiting, especially when he had done them a special deal.

"Mamm. C'mon, Richard Black is here for the

meeting," Faith said anxiously, when she caught sight of her mother in the doorway of the B&B.

When her mother turned around to look at Faith, Faith saw that she had been speaking to Verity.

"Who's Richard Black?" Verity asked.

Faith had to think fast. "Just a new supplier. We're just trying to get things a bit cheaper."

Verity looked very suspicious as she asked, "Like what?"

"Oh, Verity, I don't have time to talk about it now." Faith snapped harshly at Verity, figuring that was the only way she could put a fast end to her sister's probing questions. Verity was not one to leave things alone and Faith was concerned that Verity would insist on getting to the bottom of exactly who Richard Black really was. "Now, come on *mamm*." Faith turned and strode back to the restaurant with her mother following close behind her.

As they walked through the back door of the restaurant, Faith's mother said, "You just lied, Faith."

"I know I lied. What was I supposed to do? Did you want me to tell Verity who Richard Black is?

'Nee, but I did not want you to lie about it."

Faith felt that her heart was about to explode. She stopped still and looked straight into her mother's face. "Should I go back and tell her what trouble we are in? What would you have had me do, Mamm?" The word *'mamm'* was spoken with exaggerated irritation.

Mrs. Fisher shrugged her shoulders. "I don't know; I don't like lying, that's all. Now, we can't keep Richard waiting." Her mother floated past Faith and straight into the restaurant as if she didn't have a care in the world.

Since Faith's father had gone to be with the Lord, her mother had begun to irritate Faith immensely.

"Arrr, here you both are." Richard stood to his feet while the two women sat down at the table.

Once again, Richard could not take his eyes off Mrs. Fisher.

"So, Faith, where is the paperwork that we need for this meeting?" Mrs. Fisher asked, but then she answered her own question before Faith had a chance to speak. "Oh, I have them in the back room. Just a minute." A moment later, Faith's mother returned and handed some paperwork to Richard Black. "These are the outgoings and the incomings that the accountant did on his spread sheet thing."

It was clear to Faith that her mother did not have any idea what she was talking about and Faith wondered if Richard knew that, as well.

Richard thumbed through the pages for a few moments. Then he put the paper down in front of him and looked at Mrs. Fisher. "It's critical that you have your finger on the pulse of all the expenses at all times. This is crucial to maximize your margins."

Faith's mother nodded as if she understood clearly what he was saying.

Richard continued, "I'm no expert in restaurants, but I've done a little research with some friends of mine who own two very successful restaurants. You need to know your waste, your inventory, and your energy output. You have to run this business as lean as you possibly can." He looked from one woman to the other before he continued. "Always be on the lookout for ways to reduce costs. Whether that be in procedures, sourcing food from different places, or ways to avoid unnecessary costs." He took a sip of his hot tea that Verity had placed in front of him while he was waiting for Faith and her mother. "The days of just placing food in front of customers and doing things ad hoc are over."

"I see," Mrs. Fisher said, while fiddling with the back of her prayer *kapp*.

"I also see that you have no social media presence. No website at all and no Facebook or Twitter." Mr. Black leaned back in his chair and looked back and forth between the two women, waiting for a response.

Faith said, "Reuben has a website for bookings at the B&B."

"That's good, but the restaurant needs one as well. Before people come to an area, they research what's there. We want this restaurant to come up on their web search as the place to go to eat in Lancaster."

Faith nodded.

"Now, what do you consider that the restaurant is known for?" Richard directed his question to Faith.

Faith pondered his question for a moment. "Lunches, I'd say, mainly."

"Well, make a push on the lunches, then. My friend who owns the two restaurants said he does well out of breakfasts and in particular, from just coffees. Apparently there's a large mark-up on coffee."

"I suppose so." Faith nodded, not knowing if what he had just said was correct or not. She was not used to running a business. Last week, she was making coffees and doing a little work in the kitchen from time to time. Now, she was supposed to know about inventories, profit, and even Twitter.

"You don't know about the mark-up on coffee?" Richard Black raised his eyebrows as he almost glared at Faith.

Faith gave a little apologetic shrug of her shoulders. "I've never really worked it out."

Richard Black ran his hand through his hair quickly then brought his hand down to the table two or three times as if he were going to slice the table in two. "These are the things you must know. You shouldn't be running a business without knowing your costs."

Faith nearly cried, but fought back the tears. "This is all new to me. I never had to do anything like this before."

"It looks like you both have to co-manage this business now with Mr. Fisher not here. Is that correct?"

Faith and her mother exchanged glances then nodded simultaneously to Mr. Black.

"I'll tell you what." His eyes fixed directly on to

Faith. "For your homework for next week, find out exactly what a cup of coffee costs in a take-away cup. I want to know what the wholesale cost of the paper cup is, as well as the cost of the coffee, the milk, and the wages for the amount of time it takes someone to make the coffee. Can you do that?"

"*Jah*, of course I can."

His eyes fixed on Faith's mother. "Now, you, Mrs. Fisher. Homework for you is to accompany me to a restaurant before our next meeting."

"Oh, I can't." Mrs. Fisher suddenly leaned away from him, pushing her hands against the table.

"Mrs. Fisher, I assure you this is business for me. We need to know what the competition is doing. Don't we?"

Mrs. Fisher looked at her daughter, and Faith gave her a nod, as if to say that it was okay.

"All right," Mrs. Fisher said.

"Good. Phew, you are both such hard work. I'm glad I don't have to do this with all my clients." Richard Black looked at his obviously expensive watch. "I'm sorry, ladies, I'll have to leave you now." He looked at Mrs. Fisher, and said quietly, "Is tomorrow night all right for you?"

Mrs. Fisher smiled and nodded with her lips pressed together. It was clear to Faith that her mother did not want to go anywhere with Mr. Black.

"Good. I have your address, of course, on your paperwork. So I'll pick you up at seven." In what Faith had already come to see as his "usual" style, his words were not delivered as a question; they were a statement.

Richard left the two women sitting there as if they had just encountered a whirlwind.

"Oh, *Mamm,* I feel so inadequate. I never thought to find out such things as how much a cup of coffee costs us."

"I don't think your *vadder* would have even known that."

"How do you feel about going to dinner with him?"

Mrs. Fisher shrugged her shoulders. "Doesn't matter, does it? It's not as if I have a choice. He's only trying to help us, so we should be grateful. He certainly seems to know what he's doing."

"Jah, he certainly does." Faith was a little worried about her mother. Was Richard Black seeing his dinner date with mother as an actual date? Her mother was not used to *Englisch* men and their ways and that was concerning to Faith. Richard Black had said that it was purely business, but why was he wasting his time?

He had already loaned them money and as he said, he didn't do this with other people he had loaned money to. It all seemed a little odd.

The only thing that made sense to Faith was that Richard Black was attracted to her mother. She was a very attractive woman for her age, but surely a wealthy, handsome *Englischer*, such as Richard, would be able to have any woman he chose. Faith dared not voice her concerns to her mother; she was under enough stress as it was.

"Well, I'd better be getting back home. I've got a lot of chores to do. You'll be able to look after yourself for dinner tomorrow night, won't you?" her mother asked now.

"Jah, Mamm. I'll be able to look after myself when you're on a date." Faith giggled and tried to make light of the situation.

"Hush, Faith. Don't say such a thing, not even in a joke; someone may hear you. I don't want people to think that I'm doing that kind of thing."

Faith stopped giggling. "I'm sorry. I was only joking."

"That's all right. It just pays to look after your reputation, you know?"

"Jah, I know." Her mother had always told her, from the time Faith was quite young, that a girl's reputation was very important. The Scripture says to abstain from the appearances of evil; not just evil, but the appearance of evil.

CHAPTER 12

Let your conversation be without covetousness; and be
content with such things as ye have: for he hath said, I
will never leave thee, nor forsake thee.

Hebrews 13:5

Faith waited in the darkened house for her mother to come home from going to the restaurant with Richard Black.

It all doesn't make sense. He told us to focus on lunches and then he says we have to see what other restaurants are doing for dinners. *Why didn't he take mamm to a restaurant at lunchtime? Why at dinner?* She was sure that Richard Black was up to no good.

It was getting close to midnight and there was still no sign of Richard Black's sleek, black car. Faith waited in the sitting room and had just drifted off to sleep when the bright headlights of Richard's car shone through the sitting room windows and woke her up. Faith raced to the window, pleased that she could spy on them undetected from the darkened room.

Faith could see nothing, as his car windows were dark. She was sure that she heard her mother laughing, which was a very unfamiliar sound. Faith squinted, but still she could not see through the opaque windows of his car. Moments later, a car door opened and her mother walked quickly to the house. Richard Black turned his car in a full circle to face back up the driveway. Once her mother stood on the porch, she waved to Mr. Black, who had his window down. Faith saw him give a little wave back as his car roared up the driveway toward the road.

Faith did not want her mother to know that she

had been spying. She scrambled back to the couch so she could pretend she was asleep.

After her mother lit the gas lamp, she said, "Faith, wake up."

Faith made a broad show of waking up, stretching her arms over her head and giving a large yawn. "I must have fallen asleep. Are you back early?"

"I have no idea what time it is. Why didn't you have the lights on?"

"It's cozy in the dark. I was just waiting up for you, but I must have fallen asleep." Faith stood to her feet. "So, how did things go with Mr. Black?"

"Oh, fine. We had a very nice dinner and saw what the competition does. So it was an education."

Faith tried to read between the lines of what her mother was saying. Was her mother really seeing it as a business dinner? Or did she realize that Mr. Black was obviously hoping for something more?

Faith decided to probe a little further. "So, what do you think of him?"

"Who?"

"Richard Black, of course. What do you think of Richard Black?"

Mrs. Fisher took off her coat. "He seems to be a very clever man. That's all I know."

"What did he talk to you about?"

She shrugged her shoulders. "Nothing much, this and that. Now, I'd better be off to bed; we both have to be at the restaurant early tomorrow."

"I'm going to sit down here for a little while longer."

"Gut nacht." Her mother hung up her coat and walked up the steps to her bedroom.

Faith could not figure out if it was her imagination

or not, but she thought she noticed a spring in her mother's steps. *Surely she would not entertain even the thought of another man so soon after dat has gone. Especially not an Englischer, and especially not an Englischer like Mr. Black.*

Faith dismissed her concerns; her mother would not be interested in Mr. Black, but was Mr. Black interested in her? Maybe Mr. Black was just helping them, as he had said, and wanted nothing in return except the interest on the money he had loaned them. *Maybe he's just protecting his investment,* Faith thought. Unlike the bank, maybe he was just doing them a good deed.

* * *

At three p.m. the next day, at the restaurant,

Faith's mother said to her, "I'm heading home now, Faith. I've arranged for someone to give you a ride home."

Faith rubbed her chin and narrowed her eyes at her mother. "I can walk home; I do it all the time. Why, who have you arranged to give me a ride home?"

"I've arranged for Jakob to give you a ride home at five o'clock."

Faith put her hands on her hips and pressed her lips together firmly as she glared at her. "Why?"

"Don't be like that. I'm just being neighborly and having him over for dinner with his girls."

"Again? He was only just over for dinner."

"*Jah*, but not with his girls. I thought you should see how sweet they are."

"Why? It's nothing to do with me. I see them at all the gatherings anyway." Faith didn't mean to sound rude or callous, but she knew her mother was up to her matchmaking tricks again. Maybe Faith would have to tell her that she liked Ben Schrumb. Only Ben was not wealthy like Jakob Lapp, so her mother might not see him as a match for Faith. Anyway, it was Faith's choice and she did not appreciate her mother meddling in her life.

There was nothing at all she could do about it at this late stage except get driven home by Jakob. He called for her at the restaurant at 5 p.m. on the dot. His two daughters were in the buggy.

"Hello, Miss," they said simultaneously, as if they had been schooled to do so.

"Hello, girls." Faith searched her head for their names, but no names jumped out to her. "Now, what are your names?"

The oldest one said, "I'm Tracey and she's Lizzy."

"I'll speak for myself, Tracey."

"Too late, isn't it?" Tracey almost shouted.

The girls started to poke each other and Faith decided she had better turn her eyes to the road ahead. She had no idea what to do if they really started to hurt each other. It was obvious that they weren't as well behaved as her mother had led her to believe.

Jakob spoke above his daughters' noise. "The girls are very excited to go out to dinner. We don't do that very much these days. It was nice of your *mudder* to invite us."

"Well, she's looking forward to it. She was talking for a long time to me the other day about how sweet and lovely your girls are."

Jakob took his eyes off the road for a moment and glanced at her. "Really? She said that?"

"*Jah*, she did." Faith saw that she could do a little

matchmaking of her own if she wanted. Jakob seemed a little too pleased that Mrs. Fisher thought well of his girls.

Before Faith had driven the short distance home in the buggy, she had a headache from the girls' constant bickering. She wondered whether Jakob had noticed it or whether he thought that it was normal for them to behave so.

"I see Mrs. Fisher. I'm going to say hello to her first," said one of the girls.

"Nee, I'm going to be first," said the other.

Both girls raced out of the buggy and ran quickly to Faith's mother.

"Hush, girls, you're making such a noise," Mrs. Fisher said. "Now come in here and you can help me with dinner. Would you like that?"

Faith's mother had a special knack for having

children behave.

"*Jah*, we would," Lizzy said, while Tracey nodded.

"Hello, Jakob." Mrs. Fisher said to Jakob, as he walked through the front door behind Faith.

Faith could see this would be a very long evening. With the two girls helping her mother, she would have to sit on the couch and talk to Jakob. She had no idea what to talk to him about and after a full day and a nightmare ride in the buggy, making small talk was the last thing she wanted to do.

Thankfully, dinner was served quite quickly. Her mother handled the girls extremely well, and they did not seem to mind Mrs. Fisher chastising them as she had to once or twice during the meal.

CHAPTER 13

Take my yoke upon you, and learn of me; for I am meek and lowly in heart: and ye shall find rest unto your souls.

Matthew 11:29

"The meeting this coming Sunday was to be at our *haus,* but it's been changed to Jakob's *haus.*"

Faith and her mother always talked about things over breakfast rather than dinner, since Faith often missed dinner due to working the late shift.

"Why's that?" Faith looked up from spreading butter on her thick slice of toast.

"I'm just not up to having a meeting in the *haus.* It's just too much work for me with your *vadder* gone." Faith's mother turned her back on Faith and began to whisk some fresh eggs.

"But all the community helps, *Mamm*." Faith enjoyed having the meeting at her place. It was so much easier than hitching the buggy and driving somewhere in the early hours every second Sunday morning.

"*Jah*, but I think I'll talk to the bishop and say that I don't want any more meetings at our place. They won't miss having them here. Our turn only came about once every six months, anyway."

Faith couldn't help wondering whether the stress of having the meeting at their place was truly too much for her mother, or whether it had something to do with the sudden loss of Faith's dat. Was her mother losing a little faith in *Gott* for having her husband taken so suddenly?

"It's been a while since Jakob had a meeting at his

haus, hasn't it?"

"*Jah,* but he said he's going to start having them there again. He seems quite pleased about it. I think he took the death of his *fraa,* Janet, very hard."

"Well, I imagine it would be hard for anyone," Faith said.

"Especially hard with *kinner* to look after, but he's done extremely well with them. They're lovely girls." Faith's mother looked at Faith as if she were trying to make a point.

"*Mamm,* you may as well know that it's Ben Schrumb who I like, not Jakob."

"Ben? *Nee, nee!*" Mrs. Fisher shook her head violently. "He's no *gut.* I've heard that he's been in jail."

Faith could feel her cheeks burning with rage at her mother "That's only because he drove *dat* to the

157

hospital in a borrowed car."

"Borrowed?" Mrs. Fisher laughed. "More like stolen, wasn't it?"

"He only did it for *dat*, to get him to the hospital as fast as he could. If we had called for an ambulance, it would have taken a lot longer. He was trying to save your husband and my father." Faith was shocked as she heard her own voice screaming at her mother for the very first time in her life.

Her mother just stood there looking at Faith. Mrs. Fisher was holding a pan full of scrambled eggs in her hands and her mouth was wide open.

"So there." Faith stood up and walked out of the room. She would go without breakfast. She did not say sorry, nor did she make any excuses for her rage. In her opinion, her anger and rage against her mother were justified.

As she closed the door of her bedroom, Faith heard her mother shout from the kitchen, "I'm only thinking of you."

Faith had to smile at those words. She had to see the funny side; otherwise, she would go a little daft. She knew that she was not thinking of Faith at all. Her mother was thinking of the restaurant and of money, she was not thinking of Faith.

Faith threw herself on her bed and closed her eyes. If only things could go back to how they once were. If only her father were still alive and she could go to work without one worry in the world. Before he died, her biggest worry was how to get Ben to notice her. Now, with so many other worries and torments, Ben had fallen to last place on her agenda.

* * *

Sunday at Jakob's place arrived all too quickly and Faith and her mother had hardly spoken to each other since they had had those words over Ben.

Why can't mamm see what a gut person Ben is? Why does she keep trying to push me together with Jakob, even though he is so old?

They pulled up in the buggy just on eight a.m., when the service was due to start.

Before they got out of the buggy, her mother leaned toward Faith and whispered, "This is the best land in the county and it's well over forty acres."

Faith said nothing, just giving a little shake of her head, then turning and getting out of the buggy. She figured there wasn't much point in saying anything to her mother, as she didn't seem to hear anything Faith said these days anyway.

Mrs. Fisher began to walk very quickly. "We're

late; they're about to start."

Faith followed close behind and walked through the door of the house to see that everyone was already seated. As usual, the men were on one side and the women on the other. The only two seats left were next to Mrs. Lapp, Jakob's mother. Faith made sure her mother sat next to Mrs. Lapp, while Faith sat on the end of the bench seat. The singing began. Faith did not enjoy the singing very much on Sundays; she much preferred the lively singings the young people had in the evenings, which was very different from the Sunday singing.

From where she sat, Faith had a fairly good view of the men. She looked for Ben and saw that he was sitting next to his father in the second row from the front. Faith admired the straightness of his back and the width of his strong shoulders. Her eyes wandered to the other young men, but none of them were remarkable like Ben.

Faith also looked for Jakob, so she would be able to avoid him as soon as the service was over. He was sitting in the very back row. Faith noticed that her mother kept glancing in his direction.

As soon as the church meeting was over, several ladies hurried to the kitchen. Once everyone stood up, men arranged tables in the middle of the room for the meal.

Faith walked outside to try to escape from her mother and her obvious meddling. As soon as she walked through the front door, she noticed that Jakob was already outside and was just to her right.

"Oh, hello, Jakob."

"Hello, Faith. Have you been to my haus before?"

"I think I was here some years ago. You used to

have meetings here, didn't you, some time ago?"

"*Jah,* I did."

"It's a very fine *haus* you have."

"*Denke, Gott* has blessed me. I've inherited a fine *haus* and land."

As they were standing on the porch with a grand view of the property, Faith stood on tiptoes and said, "So, where does your land end?"

Jakob pointed to the left. "Over the other side of that creek." Then he pointed to the right. "And roughly over the other side of that road over there." Jakob chuckled a little. "I don't like to sound boastful, but if you look in front of us, it's as far as the eye can see."

"That's a lot of land."

Jakob nodded. "Developers have been after me for the creek-front land; they want to divide it into building lots."

"Oh, no, that would ruin the beautiful land so much."

Jakob folded his arms in front of his chest and smiled. "That's what I say."

Faith licked her lips. "The inside of the *haus* looks a little different from what I remember."

"I had every thing redone five years ago. New kitchen, with a bigger food storage room, new plumbing, I put amenities in the three bathrooms, and two new wood heaters. I would show you around the place, but I can't really do that today."

Ben suddenly opened the front door and then stopped, looking at the two of them before stepping back inside.

Oh dear, I hope he doesn't think that I like Jakob, Faith thought.

"So, how is your *mudder* doing?" Jakob had not noticed Ben or Faith's distress.

"She's not really been herself." That was the most polite way of saying that her mother had turned into a complete beast, and her personality had taken a turn for the worse.

"Don't worry. That's only normal. She's been through a really big shock."

So have I, Faith thought. *I've lost my dat and that must be just as traumatic; why can't people see that?*

At that moment, her mother came through the door to join them. "There you are, Faith."

"Jah, Jakob has just been telling me about his land."

"It has to be the nicest land in the county." Mrs. Fisher smiled up into Jakob's eyes.

Faith thought she saw a little something between

the two of them. It was the way they looked at each other. Her mother had to be a good ten years older than Jakob, but to look at them together you would think they were around the same age. They certainly did not look like an odd pair when they were standing together. The two of them looked as though they could be married to each other.

Faith walked inside and left the two of them on the porch. She was trying to find Ben, when old Mrs. Lapp cornered her.

Mrs. Lapp stood in Faith's way and said, "Faith, we are only a small group, but we are a *familye*. We have the same beliefs and that is what holds us together."

Faith nodded, smiled, and walked a little beyond Mrs. Lapp to take some cheese and a slice of bread from the table, which was already covered in food.

Some people sat to eat, while others preferred to stand and talk while they ate.

Faith turned away from the table with her cheese and bread, only to see that Mrs. Lapp had been waiting for her.

"How did you like what the bishop said today?" Mrs. Lapp said.

"Okay." Faith managed to speak with a mouthful of cheese.

Mrs. Lapp stepped in very close to Faith. "I think your *mudder* is glad that you're here."

Faith figured Mrs. Lapp was either having a lapse of memory, or she had Faith confused with someone else, as Faith always went to every meeting. "I suppose *mudder* is pleased."

Mrs. Lapp peered into Faith's eyes. "If you don't have *Gott,* you have nothing."

Faith nodded and stepped back a little. Staring at Mrs. Lapp's hollow cheeks, gaunt face, and the dark circles under her eyes, the sight was beginning to make Faith a little light-headed. There was talk some years ago that Mrs. Lapp was a witch. Before now, Faith had taken that to be idle gossip from a few of the young people, but now Mrs. Lapp was beginning to scare her.

"There you are, *Mamm*." Jakob put his hands on Mrs. Lapp's shoulders and steered her away from Faith.

A moment later, Jakob came back and said, "I'm sorry. She's been saying some odd things lately. I hope she wasn't rude to you or anything."

"Not at all, just talking about *Gott.*"

"I'm sure you're just being polite. Anyway, I'm sorry for anything she said to you."

Faith noticed Ben just over Jakob's shoulder. Oh

no, he's sees me talking to Jakob again. "It's okay, Jakob, really." Faith turned and headed to the other table where they were serving the hot tea.

By this time, Faith just wanted to go home. As she warmed her hands around a cup of hot tea, she looked around for her mother, but could not see her. It was half an hour before she found her and Faith was very grateful that they could head home.

When they were nearly home, her mother said, "I noticed you were speaking to Jakob a little. Have your thoughts on him changed?"

"*Nee*. I've always liked him; he seems a very nice *mann*. I don't like him as a husband, though. He's too old and I just don't have that feeling about him."

Her mother stared at her. "Love is not a feeling, Faith. Love is growing together with *Gott*. You can't wait to feel a feeling."

"Didn't you have a feeling with *dat?*"

Her mother looked straight ahead. "I can't remember; it was a long time ago."

CHAPTER 14

For God hath not given us the spirit of fear; but of power, and of love, and of a sound mind.

2 Timothy 1:7

The next day when Faith arrived to start her shift at the restaurant, she saw that Ben's buggy was parked outside. *That's funny, Lilly doesn't work today. He can't be dropping her to work. Maybe she's got her days mixed up again,* she thought.

Then Faith remembered that Lilly was married now, so it didn't make sense that Ben's buggy was there at all.

As she came closer, Lilly came out of the restaurant to meet Faith. "Guess what? I'm working instead of you today." She leaned in close and whispered. "I've arranged a surprise."

"*Nee*, Lilly. I don't like surprises. No surprises, please."

"You might like this one. I've arranged for you and Ben to spend the whole day together."

Faith felt heat race through her body. "Oh, Lilly. I said no matchmaking. I'm so embarrassed; this is all so false and, well … pushed."

Lilly threw back her head and laughed. "Nonsense, you two go and have a lovely time."

Faith saw Ben step out of his buggy.

"All right, then." Faith walked toward Ben, who had a very large smile on his face.

"Hello, Faith."

Faith climbed into the buggy. "Hello. Well, this is a surprise."

"I hope you don't mind, do you?" Ben stared at

her and waited for her to answer.

"*Nee*, not at all. I'll be better when I get over the shock. I don't usually like surprises."

Ben leaned toward her slightly and said in a low voice, "I'll have to remember that."

"I'm pleased to spend the day with you." Faith wanted to be clear to Ben that she did like him, just in case he thought otherwise.

Ben clicked his horse forward and the large bay horse responded instantly.

"It's such a beautiful day; I'll be pleased that I'm not inside today."

Ben shot her a smile. "I'm very blessed to work out doors. That is, when the sun is shining." He laughed. "Perhaps not so blessed when the rain is coming down in buckets."

Although the wind was chilly, the sun was shining

now and there were only a few small clouds near the horizon.

Half an hour later, Ben pulled up the buggy when they were on a narrow lane, surrounded by paddocks.

"Faith, I have to be honest with you."

"Yes, Ben?"

"I do like you very much, but I keep seeing you with Jakob. Is something happening with you both?"

Faith laughed just a little. She laughed only to be polite as inside she was still very angry with her mother for her meddling ways. *"Nee,* there is nothing happening with Jakob and me, or anyone else."

Ben looked down into her vivid, blue eyes. "I see the two of you together everywhere I go. Why is that?"

"We're never together. I've only spoken to him at the meeting on Sunday and then *mamm* has invited him to dinner." Faith let out a sigh. "It's my *mamm.*"

Ben put his head to one side and waited for her to continue.

"She's trying to match me with Jakob."

"Why? He's so much older than you and surely you wouldn't want to take on the burden of someone else's *kinner.*" Ben pulled a face. "I didn't mean that how it sounded; I just meant that surely that could not be a perfect situation for you."

Faith momentarily closed her eyes and put her hands over her face. "I know that, but my *mudder* doesn't seem to know that."

"Then why is she doing it?"

Faith bit on her top lip. "I didn't want to tell you this. It's quite a long story."

"Well, let's go for a walk and you can tell me everything."

After they were out of the buggy and walking

175

across the field, Faith began her story. "After *dat* died, *mamm* found out that the restaurant and the B&B were in quite a bit of strife, financially. Anyway it turns out *dat* had borrowed money, then we had to borrow more money and we are just hoping things turn around."

Ben put his chin in his hands. "And?"

"And, I suppose *mamm* thinks if she can marry me off to Jakob Lapp, then the restaurant and the B&B can be saved from ruin."

"I see." Ben was silent for a moment and looked at the ground. "I thought they were both doing very well."

"*Jah*, I did too. It had something to do with the B&B being vacant for so long after *dat* bought it. I think that drained the money away. Well, it did according to the accountant."

Ben nodded his head and looked to the ground.

"And, your mudder doesn't see me as a match for you?"

"She isn't thinking straight at all since *dat* has gone to be with the Lord. Not at all. It's like she is a different person; a person who I don't even know."

Ben turned his face to the sun and momentarily closed his eyes. "Don't be too hard on her. It must be awful for her to lose her husband, then be faced with business problems, especially when she's never had to deal with those sorts of things before."

"I suppose so." But that does not excuse her behavior, Faith thought. "It's been hard on me, too."

"I know it has." He put his hand gently on her shoulder, which sent sparks flying through her. She looked up at him and smiled into his kind eyes.

"Come this way." He pulled on Faith's arm slightly. "I'll take you to my secret place."

"You have a secret place?"

"*Jah*, I go to my secret place whenever I am upset over something or just when I want to feel closer to *Gott*."

Ben led Faith to the creek. They walked along the side of the creek a little way until they could walk no further. The undergrowth from the trees was too thick for them to pass.

Ben crouched down. "In here."

"In where?"

"My secret place is in here." Ben lifted up two tree branches to reveal a small clearing, which was room enough for someone to crawl through. "You go through first."

Faith lifted up her full dress a little, crouched down, and crawled through the narrow space. Before long, she was able to stand up and Ben stood next to her.

"See how private this is?" Ben said.

On both sides of them there was thick undergrowth but in the middle there was a clearing, which was big enough for the two of them.

"We could hide in here and no one would ever find us." Ben looked behind him. "Sit down."

There was a ledge where they could sit and watch the water babbling in front of them.

"What a perfect, heavenly place."

"*Jah,* it is. It is my secret—well, now it's our secret place."

Their shoulders were touching as they sat on the ledge. Faith turned to face Ben and at that same moment, he faced her. Ben leaned his face closer to hers and Faith leaned into him slightly until their lips touched briefly. Faith was the first to pull away, but not before she experienced small tingles of delight throughout her entire being. She felt as if she were glowing from within.

"Have you kissed any other girls?"

Ben smiled and gave a little laugh. "*Nee*, I haven't. I haven't been interested in any other girls."

Faith could feel Ben looking at her but she kept her eyes straight ahead from fear that she might let him kiss her again. It wasn't that she didn't want him to kiss her; it was because she was not sure if she should kiss him again.

"Have you kissed anyone?"

Faith laughed and shook her head. *"Nee."*

"Not Jakob Lapp?"

Faith laughed again and dug Ben in the ribs. "Don't tease me, of course not Jakob Lapp."

Ben put his strong arm around her shoulders as

they sat amongst the heavy undergrowth and watched the fast flowing water.

"You have made this perfect place even more perfect," Ben said.

This time Faith did look into his eyes and they both smiled at each other.

"So, what are we to do with your *mudder?*"

"I don't know. Should we match Jakob up with someone on our own? So *mamm* forgets about matching him up with me?"

"*Jah,* that's an idea, but who?"

They both thought for a while, but not a single woman came to mind who would suit Jakob Lapp.

Ben shook his head. "I can't think of anyone."

"Neither can I. There must be someone who would suit him."

After they sat in silence for a time, Faith said,

"Your *schweschder* said that there are some girls interested in you."

"So, you've talked to Lilly about me?"

Faith was sure that she was blushing as she nodded.

"Well, I don't know who they might be because I don't see any girls but you. I mean, they might be there, but I don't see them."

Faith's eyes fell to the ground and her lips turned up at the corners into a huge smile.

Ben drew her in tightly toward him until she could feel the hardness of his chest muscles. "What would you think if we got married?"

Faith looked into Ben's kind eyes. "Really? You want to marry me?"

"I surely do. I wouldn't have shared this secret place with you unless I thought you might say yes to me when I ask you to marry me."

Faith giggled. "I say 'yes' then. That way your secret place is safe."

"Let's get married as soon as we can."

Faith nodded and hoped that he wasn't joking.

"I've always liked you, Faith."

Faith drew back a little so she could look into his face properly. "You have? I never knew."

"Ever since you started to come to the *haus* to visit Lilly."

"That's around the time that I started to like you, too."

* * *

As Ben drove Faith back home, Faith became worried about her mother's reaction to finding out that Faith would be marrying Ben and not marrying Jakob. "Let's not tell my *mudder* just yet."

"Okay, let's tell the bishop first and then we can be announced. I want to marry you as soon as we can."

Faith's mother was in the garden tending the flowers as Ben's buggy approached. She stood up and her eyes narrowed and her lips appeared as if they were just drawn in one line.

Ben whispered. "Your *mudder* looks angry."

"I think she is."

"I'd better go now."

"Jah," was all Faith could say as she fixed her eyes upon her mother.

Ben and Faith held each other's hand for a moment before Faith left the buggy.

As Ben's horse and buggy clip clopped up the

driveway, her mother said, "I called to work and Lilly said you were with Ben. Where did you go to?"

"We just went for a walk, down by the creek."

Her mother stood staring at Faith, as if waiting for her to continue speaking.

Faith diverted her *mudder's* attention. "It's getting late. Do you want me to start the dinner?"

"Jah, that would be nice. We're having the roast chicken that was left over from last night. Just boil some vegetables to have with it, will you?"

"Sure." Faith wasn't as good a cook as her four older sisters, but she figured that was because they had all the practice, whereas she didn't have to cook that often due to being the youngest one. Cutting and boiling the vegetables was something she was capable of doing. Even though she helped prepare the food at the restaurant that was a very different thing to cooking an entire meal from start to finish. Shane was the chef at work and anything Faith did with food was always under his instructions.

Dinner was spent with Faith and her mother barely speaking to each other. Faith hoped that some time in the future she would be able to have a relationship with her mother like she used to before her father had passed. These days the only conversations between the two of them were either about work, money problems, or Jakob Lapp.

Faith took a deep breath. It was no use waiting for the right time to break the news about her and Ben. She knew that there would never be a right time so she might as well get it over with.

"*Mamm*, Ben and I plan to be married."

Mrs. Fisher dropped her fork and knife from her hands and they clanged on to the table. "Ben

Schrumb?"

"Why?"

"I'm in love with him, of course."

Mrs. Fisher dropped her eyes down to the food in front of her and shook her head. "Didn't we talk about the love feeling?" She looked up at Faith. "You can't go by feelings, feelings don't last."

"That is something that I'll have to find out for myself."

"*Nee*, Faith. That's why *Gott* gave you a *mudder*—to tell you things that you do not know."

Faith quietly placed her knife and fork on the table. "Would you feel this way if I were going to marry Jakob?"

"Well, that would be an entirely different thing."

"Why? I don't see why that would be different. Jakob doesn't even suit me. He's a lot older and he already has children."

Her face soured. "So, you've made up your mind, have you?"

"*Jah*. I wish you could be happy for me."

"Give me time, give me time." Mrs. Fisher suddenly looked up from staring into her food. "Where will you live?"

Faith hadn't even talked to Ben about where they would live. Until now, it had not seemed real and the marriage seemed as if it would take place at a distant time. "We haven't really spoken about it."

Mrs. Fisher nodded and sliced a piece of potato with her fork.

"Would you mind if we lived here for a while?" Although they were not getting on very well, Faith did not like the idea of her mother living alone. Not after having a house full just a few years ago. She had lived with five girls, her husband and her husband's mother for many years.

Her *mudder* looked up at her and said, "I suppose that might be all right if you live here."

Faith smiled. She knew that her mother would be very happy if she stayed in the house with her for a time.

After a silent moment, Mrs. Fisher said, "Don't think me horrible. I just had my heart set on you marrying Jakob and then you would never face any of these dreadful money problems like we're facing now."

"I don't think you're horrible, *mamm*. It's just that everyone has to choose their own way in life after they become a certain age. I'm nearly twenty so I'm way past being young."

"You can't blame a *mudder* for worrying about her *kinner*."

"I can actually. The Scripture says to cast all your worry upon Him for He cares for you."

Mrs. Fisher laughed. "Your *vadder* used to say that one all the time."

"I know. How do you think that I remember it?" Faith laughed and felt for the first time that her mother and herself might be starting to mend the rift that had developed between the two of them.

Mrs. Fisher clapped her hands together. "I guess we have a wedding to plan."

"*Jah*, we do."

"The last of my girls getting married." Tears came to her eyes. "I wish your *vadder* was here to see you get married. He was here to see your sisters get married."

"I'm sure he'd rather be with the Lord. You must stop thinking things that will upset you."

* * *

"Faith, let me sew your wedding dress for you," Lilly said at work a few days later.

Faith looked up from the coffee machine. "Really? You'd do that?"

"*Jah,* of course. You'll soon be my *schweschder*-in-law."

"I'd love that. You're so much better at sewing that I am."

"I can't wait. Now, what color do you want for your dress?"

"Blue, I'd like a dark blue dress. Will you come with me to choose the material?"

"*Jah,* it's so exciting. I can't wait. I'm so glad that you're going to marry Ben. My little *bruder* getting married." Lilly giggled. "Now Esther is upset that she doesn't have a beau. She wanted to get married before Ben and now this has spoiled her plans."

"Who does she like?"

"No one. She hasn't found anyone she likes at all. She might have to wait until someone visits from somewhere. Maybe someone will come to your wedding. Wouldn't that be funny if she met someone at your wedding Ben?" Lilly was speaking faster than Faith had ever heard her. It was clear she was very excited at the news of her best friend's impending marriage to her *bruder*.

Then customers entering the restaurant interrupted them; it was drawing near to their busiest time of day.

CHAPTER 15

Looking unto Jesus, the author and finisher of our faith; who for the joy that was set before him endured the cross, despising the shame, and is set down at the right hand of the throne of God.

Hebrews 12:2

Faith had Verity and Lilly as her attendants and they both arrived at seven a.m. on the morning of the wedding to help Faith get ready.

"Lilly, I didn't think I would be getting married so soon after you."

"Well, I did. I knew for the longest time that you and Ben were perfect for each other."

"You did push us together."

Lilly nodded her head. "*Jah,* I did."

"Even though I asked you not to."

"Faith, I couldn't wait for the two of you to do it by yourselves. I was watching Ben at my wedding and he hardly spoke to you."

"We did talk to each other a little at the end of your wedding. He even asked to drive me home. That didn't happen, though, because of what happened with dat."

Lilly's face broke into a smile. "You never told me that."

"Didn't I? Well, my whole life kind of spiraled out of control for a while there."

Verity had been quiet for a while, but chose now to speak up. "How did things spiral out of control?"

Faith raised one shoulder. "Nothing, really."

"Why do I get the feeling that something is going on that you and *mamm* aren't telling me?" Verity folded her arms across her chest.

"It's nothing. Now, don't ruin my day by speaking to me harshly." Faith looked around her bedroom. "Lilly, did you forget my dress?"

Lilly gasped and put her hand to her mouth. "I left it downstairs. I won't be even a moment."

Lilly brought back Faith's wedding dress, along with the two attendant's dresses that she had also made.

"*Denke* for making the dresses, Lilly. I would never have been able to make them as well as you did."

Verity said, "They're beautifully made, Lilly."

Lilly smiled as she looked at the dresses.

"Well, we had better put them on if we don't want to be late." Verity was always the one to do the organizing.

The three girls changed into their dresses to the

sound of buggies arriving.

Once Faith was in her dress, she began to cry. This was the most important day in her life so far and her father was not there to share it with her. Nothing seemed the same. Her father had left a huge hole in her life. A hole that she knew that no one else could fill, not even Ben. The girls tried to comfort her.

"*Nee*, I'm all right." As soon as she uttered the words, Faith realized that they were the exact same words her father had spoken to her before he died— 'I'm all right.' Maybe her father was with her in some way. Although the words were common words, they were accompanied with a special feeling in Faith's heart as if *Gott* had her whole life in His hands. She knew that her father would have approved of Ben as her husband.

The girls came downstairs to a roomful of people.

Ben came striding toward Faith and she desperately wanted to touch him, or to at least hold his hand, but she would have to wait until they were alone. Her face started to ache from smiling at him so much.

The wedding service began with a minister teaching from the Bible. The bishop spoke over Ben and Faith of the importance of marriage and the importance of the family unit. He then pronounced that they were married. They sat back down and three hymns were sung.

The wedding meal was next on the order of service. Faith and Ben sat at the main wedding table with their attendants on either side. It was only when she was seated that she noticed that Richard Black was at her wedding. She whispered to Ben, *"Mamm* must have invited Mr. Black."

"The loan shark?"

Faith giggled. "Oh, Ben, he's a very nice man. He's not a loan shark."

"Lilly, that's what private lenders are called. Because if people don't pay up, they send people after them."

"What?"

Ben laughed. "Don't worry. I'm sure he's not like that from what you've told me, but some of them are. You have to be careful."

Mr. Black was eating at a separate table with Shane, the chef from the restaurant, and about six other *Englischers*.

Faith observed that her mother was speaking to Jakob Lapp, and Richard Black was staring at the two of them while he ate his food.

"Is he staring at your *mamm?*" Ben whispered in Faith's ear.

"You noticed, too?" Faith was pleased that she wasn't letting her imagination run away with her. Richard Black was romantically interested in her mother

"And look at the way Jakob is leaning in toward her while he's talking to her. It appears she has more than one man interested in her." Ben's eyes were drawn back to Faith.

"It is so weird to think of *mamm* with another man when *dat* has only just gone."

"Be prepared, Faith. It very well could happen." Ben put his fingers under Faith's chin and turned her face toward him. "Faith, I don't want to speak about your *mudder* or anyone else. This is our day and I'm looking forward to spending every day of the rest of my life with you."

Faith looked into his eyes and fought back the

tears that were welling up in her own eyes. "*Gott* has blessed me so much, I can barely contain my happiness."

Ben leaned in closer to her and said in a low voice. "I want all your days to be as happy as this one. I'll do everything I can to make sure that you are the happiest *fraa* alive."

Faith laughed. "And I'll do all I can to make you the happiest *mann*."

Ripples of excitement shivered through Faith's body as Ben leaned in close to her.

Ben whispered softly in her ear. "I can't wait to kiss your lips."

Faith smiled and hoped no one was looking at them speaking so intimately. She quickly scanned the room and saw that all the guests were busy eating or talking.

Ben lowered his eyes and Faith followed his gaze under the table, where he had his hand outstretched, waiting for hers. She lowered her hand under the table, placing it into his.

Faith and Ben looked into each other's eyes and smiled.

"I will thank *Gott* every day for bringing you into my life." Ben squeezed her hand and gazed into her eyes. "I love you, Mrs. Schrumb."

A warm glow, such as Faith had never known, filled her entire body from head to toe. "And I love you." Faith was grateful that her new husband, the quiet and shy Ben Schrumb, had finally found his voice.

THE END

Thank you for your interest in

'Faith's Love'

Amish Wedding Season Book 3

To be notified of Samantha Price's

NEW RELEASES and GIVEAWAYS

subscribe at:

http://www.samanthapriceauthor.com

The next book in this series is:

THE TRIALS OF MRS. FISHER

Amish widow, Abigail Fisher, is consumed with anger as she copes not only with the loss of her husband, but his poor business decisions regarding their two family businesses. As she struggles to maintain the businesses financially, Richard Black, the wealthy money lender, comes to her rescue, but is he interested in more than interest payments?

Can a humble Amish man capture Abigail's heart when she thinks that money is the only answer to her problems? Is Abigail Fisher able to rid herself of anger and bitterness to see the happiness that is offered to her, before it is too late?

Samantha loves to hear from her readers.

Connect with Samantha Price at:

samanthaprice333@gmail.com

http://twitter.com/AmishRomance

Made in the USA
San Bernardino, CA
09 December 2016